Praise for the Blood-Thirs

The Adventure of the Inco

On 2017 Recommended Reading
Tangent Online;

"[A] brisk novella...it draws deeply from the well of
19th and early 20th century speculative literature. In that
much, it reminds me no small part of Penny Dreadful.
It has the same gleeful delight in its own references, the
same playfully gothic geekery."

—Liz Bourke, *Tor.com*

"[G]rand and smashing recursive steampunk…a
splendid romp indeed."

—Paul Di Filippo, *Asimov's*

"Ward deftly incorporates details that heighten the realism of
Harker's bizarre cross-genre world, from Harker's dismissal of
classism, to the clean energy of the Martian-inspired Titanic
engines. Lucy's philosophical musings and delectable vocabu-
lary recall the style of Sir Arthur Conan Doyle while delving
into questions of emotion and personhood, responsibility and
morality, in a way that emphasizes the dehumanization of the
other—the other species, the other class, the other gender."

—Michelle Ristuccia, *Tangent Online*

The Adventure of the Dux Bellorum

"[A] gleeful mashup of historical and fictional
characters...all good fun, not without more serious
rumination on issues like colonialism and women's
suffrage."

—Rich Horton, *Locus*, April 2019

"This tale of two monsters, at once romantic and
action-packed, is fun and thought-provoking, giving
readers everything they want."

—*Publisher's Weekly* (starred review)

"[T]he book takes all the elements of the first installment and builds on it. The action is more visceral, the cast larger, the stakes much higher. There are sapient dinosaurs, vampire vs. wolfman fights, and a particularly evil German scientist who just won't seem to die. Plus there are moments where the characters must confront their missions and the legacies of their nations…."

—Charles Payseur, *Quick Sip Reviews*

The Adventure of the Naked Guide
"Cynthia Ward's Lucy Harker novellas give the modern reader an updated frolic through avant-garde genre fiction, a frolic frosted with a myriad of clever fandom-esque references sure to delight adventurous readers."

—Michelle Ristuccia, Tangent, February 2020

"Cynthia Ward continues her "Blood-Thirsty Agent" series with *The Adventure of the Naked Guide*, in which Lucy Harker, Dracula's daughter and so a dhampir, and her lover Clarimal Stein, an upiór, find themselves in Lutha, helping the British free that somewhat "Ruritanian" country from Austrian domination. … There's some exciting steampunkish action, but the story turns more on what she learns about her mothers, what she and Clarimal come to understand about their own relationship, and the implications of their work for the British Empire. This is enjoyable, as all of these stories have been…. The main purpose is more serious now (as long hinted)…

—Rich Horton, *Locus* 2020

The Adventure
of the Golden Woman

Conversation Pieces

A Small Paperback Series from Aqueduct Press
Subscriptions available: www.aqueductpress.com

About the Aqueduct Press
Conversation Pieces Series

The feminist engaged with sf is passionately interested in challenging the way things are, passionately determined to understand how everything works. It is my constant sense of our feminist-sf present as a grand conversation that enables me to trace its existence into the past and from there see its trajectory extending into our future. A genealogy for feminist sf would not constitute a chart depicting direct lineages but would offer us an ever-shifting, fluid mosaic, the individual tiles of which we will probably only ever partially access. What could be more in the spirit of feminist sf than to conceptualize a genealogy that explicitly manifests our own communities across not only space but also time?

Aqueduct's small paperback series, Conversation Pieces, aims to both document and facilitate the "grand conversation." The Conversation Pieces series presents a wide variety of texts, including short fiction (which may not always be sf and may not necessarily even be feminist), essays, speeches, manifestoes, poetry, interviews, correspondence, and group discussions. Many of the texts are reprinted material, but some are new. The grand conversation reaches at least as far back as Mary Shelley and extends, in our speculations and visions, into the continually created future. In Jonathan Goldberg's words, "To look forward to the history that will be, one must look at and retell the history that has been told." And that is what Conversation Pieces is all about.

L. Timmel Duchamp

Jonathan Goldberg, "The History That Will Be" in Louise
Fradenburg and Carla Freccero, eds., *Premodern Sexualities* (New
York and London: Routledge, 1996)

Additional Titles in the
Blood-Thirsty Agent Series

Note: To read free samples, link to each book's web-page from the author's page at Aqueduct Press, *http://www.aqueductpress.com/authors/CynthiaWard.php*

Conversation Pieces
Volume 81

The Adventure of the Golden Woman

Book 4: Blood-Thirsty Agent Series

by
Cynthia Ward

Published by Aqueduct Press
PO Box 95787
Seattle, WA 98145-2787
www.aqueductpress.com

ISBN: 978-1-61976-216-9

Cover illustration courtesy Joe Murphy
Images: British flag, Ilyabolotov/istockphoto.com;
City, Rustic/stock.adobe.com

Original Block Print of Mary Shelley by Justin Kempton:
www.writersmugs.com

Printed in the USA by Applied Digital Imaging

Acknowledgments

For their assistance and support, I'd like to acknowledge my late mother and thank my father, my sister, my brother-in-law, Steven J. Bigwood, Jessica "Jessie Lou" Butterfield, L. Timmel Duchamp, Win Scott Eckert, C.C. Finlay, Kim Fletcher, Dr. Donald M. Frazee, Lucas Garrett, Arrate Hidalgo, Dr. Kyung H. Lee, Saabrina Mosher, S., Nisi Shawl, Kathryn Wilham, Amy Wolf, and especially Dr. James Ray Comer, Angelica Figueroa, Betty Heselton, Rebecca McFarland Kyle, and Joe Murphy.

All mistakes are mine.

For Dr. J. Comer, without whom I would not have dared this series of adventures

Whence, I often asked myself, did the principle of life proceed? It was a bold question, and one which has ever been considered as a mystery; yet with how many things are we upon the brink of becoming acquainted, if cowardice or carelessness did not restrain our inquiries.

—Mary Shelley, *Frankenstein* (1818)

To think of these stars that you see overhead at night, these vast worlds which we can never reach. I would annexe the planets if I could; I often think of that. It makes me sad to see them so clear and yet so far.

—Cecil Rhodes, The Last Will and Testament of Cecil John Rhodes

When once your point of view is changed, the very thing which was so damning becomes a clue to the truth.

—Arthur Conan Doyle, "The Problem of Thor Bridge"

Berlin, Prussia, German Protectorate, 17 January 1931

In its wisdom, the British Empire ignores its pressure valves, legal and illegal: the brothels, jazz clubs, dance halls, pansy clubs, cafés, cabarets, and the rest. Berlin has as many valves as London. I'm bound for one: an unlicensed bar called the Lady Windermere.

On this subject, at least, the dossier I received in London proves accurate. The place is just off the Tauentzienstrasse. The space is packed with artists and other undesirables. The décor is Left Bank.

Though I've arrived an hour early, I've been preceded by the man who runs Station G. He faces the small stage, forelocks half obscuring his view of the expressionless chanteuse butchering the German language. I've never seen the man before, but the Secret Intelligence Service dossier included a studio portrait and several candid snapshots, so I recognise my mission supervisor immediately. But as I check my overcoat, I make a point of staring at him and blinking, as if trying to get a better look through the dim light and layered smoke.

Finally, I bend my steps to the small table, where he sits with claret-cup and cigarette, and call out in English. "Christopher! Lord above. Is that *you?*"

Under normal circumstances, I wouldn't know my mission supervisor's true name, and an invert wouldn't have any position whatsoever within the Empire's Secret Intelligence Service. Sometimes, however, it's best to hide an agent in plain sight. The director of Station G, based in the decadent German capitol, is an openly homosexual writer.

At my call, he turns his head. Squinting in my direction, he brushes the dark hair from his right eye. His expression changes to one of amazed recognition, although he knows me only from my dossier.

"Lucy Strong?" he exclaims.

On this mission, as on most, I operate under a *nom de guerre*. I'm entirely too well known in the Empire to do otherwise. I'm Lucy Harker, the legal daughter of the reputed slayer of Dracula, and the stepdaughter of Sherlock Holmes's smarter brother.

"I can't believe my eyes!" my new supervisor says, rising to clasp my hand with the warmth one reserves for a long-lost friend.

Christopher shows no reaction to being almost a head shorter than me. He's slight and wiry, with an outsized head, long arms, and short legs. With his smooth pink complexion and boyish grin, he looks closer to twenty than thirty. He smells pleasantly of wine and borage and Turkish tobacco.

His deceptively innocent smile widens. "I thought you'd run away to London to elope."

"It didn't work out," I merrily reply, "so I've run away to Berlin to write."

The singer, a woman with short black hair and a dead-white face, is no longer expressionless. She's staring at us as if I've begun making love to her husband. However, she's stuck on the stage. She's already wrapped the garrotte of her vocal cords around a new song (this one's mostly in pellucid English, obviously her native language).

Christopher releases my hand. "It's so wonderful to see you."

He offers to remove my jacket, though he must know I'll refuse. It conceals a firearm.

This is not to say the Walther PPK in my shoulder holster is my only weapon. I've a British Navy jack knife in one pocket of my jacket, a skeleton grip Beretta .25 in the other, and a Webley .25 in my garter holster. Add a Tommy gun and you might suppose I'm a gangster.

A serving girl takes my order for an Ohio cocktail. As she departs, Christopher draws back a chair for me. When I'm seated, he extends a packet of Salem Aleikum cigarettes.

I take one. "Thank you."

Striking a match, he leans close. As he lights my cigarette, his hands linger on mine. My eyes hold his gaze.

Then, my head still lowered, I glance about the space.

Our performance seems to have convinced the singer, whose enormous eyes are riveted on us. A few patrons regard us with raised eyebrows. As the dossier said, Christopher's proclivities are known here. That only makes our charade more convincing. Berlin is so dissolute, heterosexuals sleep with the same sex and homosexuals with the opposite.

As Christopher settles in his chair, I exhale smoke. "I understand you teach writing?"

"I *am* scraping by as a teacher," he says, "but of the English language, I fear."

I lean back, raising my cigarette. "If you're scraping by," I say, "I daresay it's time to expand your subject matter."

The singer puts "Mein Herr" out of its misery and makes her way through the crowded bar, exchanging greetings or flirtations with nearly every male she passes. As single-minded as a bullet, she moves in our direction. I realise her thickly powdered face and heavily made-up eyes have led me to overestimate her age by somewhere between five years and two decades. She's nineteen or twenty. A black beauty mark perches like a little round bug on one cheek, and her green fingernails resemble the bright hard chitin of tiger beetles. Her eyes, whenever she glances our way, are candidly curious.

"I shouldn't care to charge an old friend for writing advice," Christopher tells me. "Why don't we exchange typescripts?"

"I should be happy to trade editorial suggestions," I reply, "if that's what you mean."

"You know—" Christopher leans forward "—I know a writer who's in contact with several literary agents, both here and abroad. Dolf might be able to find you an agent. At the very least, he might be interested in exchanging typescripts with you. He writes in German, though."

"I'm fluent."

"Very good," Christopher says. "I'll talk to Dolf—"

"Dolf Hiedler?" The white-faced singer's accent is posh as double cream, but fails to drown the hint of Lancashire bourgeoisie.

Appropriating a chair from the table of an elderly, well-tailored Hebrew preoccupied with lighting a fresh Eckstein from the stump of his old, she seats herself at our table.

"Oh, Christopher darling," she says, as she helps herself to one of his cigarettes. "Dolf's a nasty sort, for all his love of his adopted country."

Christopher lights her gasper and provides introductions. "Lucy, this is Sally Bolle, my dearest friend in Berlin. Sally, this is Lucy Strong, an old friend from London." He cocks his head at me. "Dolf's Austrian. Although how Sally knows anything about his manner, I couldn't say."

"*Everyone* knows he's Austrian, darling," Sally replies, as if he's addressed her. Her husky contralto is pleasant, now she's not singing. "And *everyone* knows he hates the Jews worse than any German. If Germany weren't part of the British Empire, he'd be agitating against Jews instead of English sympathizers."

I elevate my eyebrows. The young lady's not addressing a covert political gathering, or fulminating behind a pen name. Addressing such blatantly indiscreet talk to a complete stranger isn't much more sensible than punching a lion in the nose.

"I cannot see how anyone in Germany can speak against the British Empire," I say. "If we hadn't stabilised the rule of the Kaiser, Germany would have collapsed following the Great War. And if it weren't for our wars against China and the United States, the whole of the Continental economy would be in shambles. Instead, nearly every man in Europe is employed."

"Sweet, I've no doubt everything would be a perfect shambles." The girl's tone indicates the matter is more dry and remote than the Martian sea-bottoms.

As she turns back to Christopher, a member of the Berliner Polizei enters the Lady Windermere with a

Luger on his gun-belt. He's followed by a mechanical man which carries a Mauser rifle at right shoulder arms. The mechanical's iron exterior is enameled in the same shade of blue as the Polizist's uniform.

The Berlin police don't share the British Empire's *laissez-faire* attitude towards unlicensed bars. And the Lady Windermere attracts *demi-mondaine* sorts: transvestites, poets, prostitutes, homosexuals, Lesbians, Negroes, Jews, communists, gangsters—there's even an artist in cowboy togs sketching a vampire with an anaemic-looking thrall. The cop and machine-man affect the patrons like a stone flung in a pool, sending awareness outward in ripples of tightened shoulders and averted faces.

Christopher matches my indifferent response to the newcomers. Sally stares openly at the mechanical, which would be a rare sight even in London. When its master begins quietly discussing protection money with the one-handed barman, she turns back to Christopher and me. Tilting her bowler hat back on her bob, she flashes a smile as friendly as a sabre blade.

"Have you heard about the golden woman?"

"Not a word," Christopher says. "Is that a new torch singer or female impersonator?"

I'm tempted to ask if the phrase refers to an infamous gold-digger, but I suspect Sally might decide I'm referring to her.

She looks at me. "You haven't heard of the golden woman, either?" When I shake my head, she exhales smoke with a laugh. "But she's all the rage, sweet! A gilded Maschinenmädchen, glimpsed from the corner of people's eyes."

"A machine maiden?" I glance at the uniform's metal companion. "Mechanicals look like men."

This is a generous assessment. Mechanicals resemble petrol barrels affixed with primitive approximations of limbs and heads. One might suppose them to be a poor, speechless parody of male mortals. In truth, they're inventions of a German scientist, Herr Doktor Krüger, whose hope of creating an army immune to Allied machine-gun fire came a cropper in the Great War.

"Perhaps the golden woman is an hallucination," Sally says. "Most of Berlin suffers from narcomania." She crushes the stump of her cigarette in a glass ash-tray with edges which could slit a throat, then turns to me with a slow, unfriendly smile. "Are you chasing Chris?"

I dispose of my own gasper.

"Certainly not," I assure her. "We're just good friends." My reply couldn't sound more insincere.

Christopher smiles at me. "Come by tomorrow afternoon, Lucy. Bring one or two of your stories. I should be delighted to read them." He gives a time and an address.

The tall, gaunt Hebrew at the next table leans towards us. I rarely smoke unless required by my cover, because it dulls my taste-buds and nose. To preserve them, I barely tasted my cigarette; but the man's smell of accumulated tobacco smoke is so overwhelming, my sensitive nose goes dead in self-defence.

Focusing pale eyes on Sally like a rifle scope, he speaks in a hoarse voice, tinged with a Warsaw accent. "Für mich, Sie sind schön, Fräulein. Darf ich Sie auf ein Getränk einladen?"

"Ganz genau!" she answers, as falsely bright as a Tannenbaum ornament, and moves to his table.

When I exit the Lady Windermere, it's nearly midnight, with a wind keen enough to scrape deerskin. Still, the streets are as busy as midday. My nose is mercifully dulled to the myriad stinks of Berlin air, but my ears receive the full assault: motor-lorries and locomotives and horse-drawn charabancs; bells and sirens and horns; jazz and cabaret and laughter and radio programmes from briefly opened doors; come-ons of beggars and vendors and street-walkers; polyglot conversations climbing to be heard. It's an atonal symphony to wrack Schönberg with envy.

Surveillance reveals no loiterer, which might suggest I'm being followed. There's a tripod nearby, towering over the Wittenbergplatz like the support for a new elevated railway. The lights of the street and U-Bahn station gleam jovially on the underside of the metal hood. The underside is enameled in the colours of the Union Jack.

As I walk east, I see another "Martian" style fighting-machine in the distance. This tripod is painted with the eagle and Schwarz-Rot-Gold of Deutschland, but make no mistake. It, too, serves the British Empire.

Berlin, 18 January 1931

Christopher barely has time to take my typescript and re-move my overcoat before Sally descends on us. She tries the doorknob of his rented room. Finding it locked, she rattles it several times, as if that must shift the tumblers. Then she pounds on the door, calling in that voice which seems much too deep for her pixie form.

"Christopher, you simply *must* let me in. I have the most terrific hangover!"

From the moment her hand touched the doorknob, my supervisor's had no doubt who's come to call. He gestures me onto the edge of his bed, his eyebrows shaping a question. At my nod, he puts his lips to mine (and for all his lack of interest, he's a quite good enough kisser to strike a spark). As he turns away, he disarrays his forelocks, and I muss the waves of my bob. Tugging a corner of his shirt from his trousers for a final louche touch, he turns the key in the lock.

Before he can grasp the knob, the door flies open. Sally bursts into his room like a runaway tram, cigarette raised in her nicotine-stained hand.

"Darling, you simply must make me a—"

She stops. She stares at Christopher's red-smeared lips and tousled appearance, as if she's seen something improbable, like a Venusian at the wheel of a Bugatti. Then she studies my disordered locks and smudged lip-stick, as if I'm even more fantastically unlikely.

"Oh, sweet," she says, with a peculiar mix of pity and delight. "Tell me you're not in love with Chris."

"I—"

She interrupts me. "I don't want to break your heart, Lucy, but better now than later. You're simply not the right sort of woman for our friend. Even *I'm* not, and I've bedded any number of homosexual men."

"Sally!" Christopher is sincerely shocked, yet he laughs.

"Don't worry about your inclinations, darling," Sally tells him. "German law may forbid unnatural fornication between persons of the male sex, but the Prussian police never enforce it. They're only concerned with traitors and subversives and bomb-throwing radicals. As long as a man avoids extremist politics, he may have all the boys he wants here. I mean, that's why you live in Berlin, Chris darling. Isn't it?"

She draws luxuriously on her cigarette and turns to me.

"Don't worry, Paragraph 175 has never applied to Sapphism," she assures me. "I mean, if your interests don't begin and end with men."

"Sally," Christopher says, laughing again, "you needn't worry about Miss Strong's romantic prospects. She's not come to Germany in search of love. She's another escapee from the dreary London literary clime."

Christopher understands our superiors haven't provided him with my real name, just as I understand there's no possibility of physical attraction on his side.

Still, most of what he's been told about me is true. I'm attracted to men (and androgynes and women, though my dossier doesn't mention this, or the woman with whom I share more than a London flat). I was a volunteer nurse and ambulance driver in the Great War (though he won't have been told I'm Dracula's ageless dhampir daughter and need cosmetics to look forty).

I've played the restless dilettante since before England completed its boa constrictor's swallowing of Europe and the Near East. I'm a peripatetic literary dabbler of marginal talent, who receives a stipend from my well-born and well-compensated stepfather.

The truth is the best cover for an undercover operative.

Sally exclaims, "Why are we chattering, when my head is absolutely bursting? I simply *must* have a prairie oyster!"

As Christopher reaches for the Worcestershire sauce, Sally seats herself next to me, releasing a puff of stale cigarette smoke from her clothing. Her head is bare, but her sleek black bob cups her skull like a helmet.

"Enchanted to see you again, sweet!" Her pale brown eyes, already big in their black make-up, become huge with sincerity. Gesturing at the table with her cigarette, she indicates the two short piles of typescript. "Are those some of Christopher's stories?" She pouts, the expression negated by the self-mockery in her eyes. "He never lets me read them."

"They're excerpts from one of my stories and one of Lucy's," Christopher corrects. "She and I are exchanging scenes to offer suggestions. I'm sure you'd find them dreadfully boring, Sally."

She helps herself to the typescripts and begins skimming. They're stories. Nothing more.

"I'm sure you're right." She discards the typescripts as if she's realised they're used lavatory paper, then snaps the glass from Christopher's hand like a £100 note. "*Thank* you, darling. I simply couldn't survive another minute without a prairie oyster." She empties the glass in a swallow and shoves it back in his direction. "Another."

Christopher shakes his head, but complies with a smile.

A telephone bell begins ringing elsewhere in the flat as Sally extinguishes her gasper. "Did I tell you I have a new man?" she asks Christopher. "After you left last night, I spent the evening making love to that horrid old Jew. He owns a department store on the Tauentzien-strasse, but simply *wouldn't* take me home! I thought I'd entirely wasted my time, but his grandnephew was in the bar the whole time—an Englishman, can you believe? He came up and offered to buy me a nightcap!" She gives me a yellow smile and confides, "He was *far* better looking than the old man, and he absolutely knows how to make love." She returns her raccoon-eyed regard to Christopher. "He said he'd call me this afternoon."

As if on cue, their landlady's voice comes through the open doorway. "Fraulein Bolle, das Telefon für Sie!"

An expression of anxiety softens the porcelain mask of Sally's face as if it were wax, and she rushes from the room.

Christopher locks his door with the alacrity of a gaoler. He puts a record on his gramophone and turns the crank, then sets the needle in the groove. From the horn comes Louis Armstrong's Hot Five, playing "Ain't Misbehavin'-Fox Trot."

It's safe now to talk in low voices, but we still sit close to one another on his bed and put our heads together.

"I intended to handle your intelligence myself," Christopher murmurs, "but an emergency's come up. I meant to inform you at the Lady Windermere, but Sally interrupted."

"What is the emergency?"

"I must leave for Switzerland at once."

My eyebrows rise. "Leave, with the King of England arriving at any moment to visit his dear cousin, Wilhelm II?"

"And half of SIS assigned to Germany for the duration?" Christopher smiles grimly. "It seems one of my agents—let's call him Mr Norris—has been transmitting information in the wrong direction. I need to handle this personally."

"I was wondering why you suggested dragging a third party into our interactions."

"Unfortunately, I must," Christopher says. "Unless you feel your information for our mutual friends can wait?"

I grimace. "Time is of the essence."

"As when is it not," he says. "I've already arranged a meeting between you and Hiedler this evening."

He provides a time and location, then shows me a snap of Hiedler, which I hope for the man's sake is unduly unflattering.

"Very good," I say. "May I trust Hiedler with everything?"

"Yes," Christopher says.

"Positively everything?"

"Everything you would share with me," he says with quiet intensity, "you should share with him."

When the needle begins scraping round the record label, I rise from the bed and speak with the breathlessness of a woman recently pleasured. "Sorry I have to dash, Christopher. I hope you have a lovely time in Switzerland."

"I rather fear I shan't." He smiles. "While I'll be staying with a gentleman friend at a winter sport resort, I haven't a clue how to skate or ski. Nor any desire to learn."

Exiting Nollendorfstrasse 17, I stay in the shadow of the doorway and surveille my surroundings. It's a calm, clear afternoon, and there are several people about. No one is lingering, which suggests I'm not being tailed; but a few pedestrians tilt their heads skyward in response to the abrupt gesture of a chestnut roaster. I follow her pointing finger.

The years seem to evaporate. For a moment, I'm back in the Hollow Earth, gaping at the planetoid which orbits its central sun.

Then I realise what I'm seeing.

The *HMS Victoria* has arrived in Berlin on its official maiden voyage, bearing George V from London.

I imitate the people on the pavement, staring at the *Victoria* as if I've never seen it before. It's the world's first and only flying aircraft carrier, and it was constructed at the secret Royal Air Force research centre on the Baltic island of Usedom. But it's difficult to keep an aerial aircraft carrier secret, and as the pedestrians begin muttering, few sound surprised. Many sound angry.

Someone shouts, "Ein englische Flugplatz!"—an English flying field. In either language, it's a pun, but the resulting laughter is as scarce and uneasy as a green maple leaf in January.

The streamlined hull is painted from bow to stern with an immense Union Jack, which obscures a multitude of bay doors and gun turrets. But obscuring details isn't the paint job's only function, as the pedestrians have realised. And in Germany, as elsewhere in British territory, the English are not popular.

The *Victoria* isn't close, but it's almost ten acres in size, so it looks closer. It seems almost to overhang the Kurfürstendamm.

The aircraft carrier is powered by an atomic engine and buoyed by eighth-ray technology. Trailing bright puffs of green smoke, the carrier makes no sound beyond the deep drone of great propellers at the stern. In a sky aswarm with aëroplanes, the carrier seems the size of a small moon.

I was eleven when the "Martians" (as we thought them then) invaded England. No matter how long I live, I shan't forget the terror and helplessness and bleak wonder of those days. Yet I cannot say Earth has seen anything more awe-inspiring or more terrifying than the *HMS Victoria*.

Britain plans construction of more air-borne aircraft carriers.

Dolf Hiedler is a dark, middle-aged Austrian whose sour face suggests a preserved lemon with a toothbrush moustache. When he draws near my table at the Eldorado, I recognise his scent; he was a Bavarian despatch motor-cyclist during the Great War. I don't remind him of our encounter.

We haven't time to order before he's handing me a sheaf of pages and addressing me in German. "Herr Christoph has told me of your generous offer to read my little piece, Fraulein Strong."

I would infinitely prefer to watch my favourite performer, the gorgeous American Negress Josephine Baker, finish singing "J'ai Deux Amours," but I bend to Hiedler's typescript.

It's a paranoid rant about Jews secretly controlling the British Empire, but it contains coded information about a Prussian baron who is leaking information to the French. The French have about as much chance of leaving the British Empire as I have of flying to Mars by flapping my arms. However, SIS will swat the baron like a gnat. No enemy spies are too small to suborn or eliminate.

And, by betraying a fellow enemy of England, I shall maintain my reputation as a trustworthy agent of the British Empire.

The orchestra is striking up to herald the arrival of female impersonator Hansi Sturm when I finish reading. I offer Hiedler a neutral observation which might be taken as praise for his writing.

"You make a most forceful argument, Herr Hiedler."

He smiles. "I'm grateful you are pleased. Grateful, too, that Herr Christoph did not send us to the Lady Windermere." When I raise inquiring brows, he explains. "Sally Bolle doesn't sing at the Eldorado. Although I assure you, Fraulein—" he looks about, his expression tightening "—I'd never have chosen this degenerate place for our *rendez-vous*."

He regards the performer and our fellow patrons with the expression of a particularly prudish prune. Though popularly viewed as a den of transvestite prostitutes, the Eldorado attracts people from every sex and walk of life, and this evening the aristocrats, bourgeoisie, and tourists are all well represented. There are also *demi-mondaine* sorts, but it's an unexceptional assemblage for a club in the Schöneberg district, and Hiedler ought not to be surprised. Perhaps he's merely constitutionally constipated.

"A crowd like this one has its uses," I murmur to Hiedler, and reach into my portfolio.

I'm facing the entrance, so I see Sally Bolle enter the nightclub. She has acknowledged the January cold to the extent of donning a beret the colour of a canary and a fur coat as patchy as an old dog. As she checks the coat, she notices us.

"Herr Heidler?" she exclaims.

Hurrying to our table, she offers the scowling man her beetle-nail hand, in vain.

Undeterred, she lowers her arm and effuses, "Such a pleasure to meet you at last!" Her German is so atrocious, I wonder if she mangles it deliberately. "Herr Christoph says you're quite the most remarkable writer he's ever read."

"I'm sure he does," I add.

Our ambiguity sails as far over Hiedler's head as the *HMS Victoria*. His scowl transforms into a smile, and he rises from his seat. As he bows to us in the Prussian manner, complete with heel-click, he says, "It's an honour to win the approval of fellow Aryans."

I'm half Irish, I've bobbed my wavy black hair, and I've powdered my dark face. But some things can't be changed so easily, and my aquiline features and the colour and shape of my eyes betray my father's Oriental blood. However, Hiedler seems willing to overlook these details. I expect Christopher has vouched for my non-existent Anglo-Saxon blood in the strongest possible terms. Whatever the case, I must suppress amusement at Hiedler's racial pride. He looks no more Aryan than I.

A waiter appears to solicit Hiedler's and Sally's orders. Sally quickly accepts my offer to share my bottle of

Orsinian Blaufränkisch. Hiedler frowns at our debauchery and orders soda water.

"I fear I shan't be staying late," I tell them when the waiter has departed. "I've an early student tomorrow," I lie, and give Sally a smile. "Christopher's set me up with an English language student who insists on a woman instructor." Placing Hiedler's typescript in my portfolio, I ask him, "Have you any other writing you'd like me to read?"

"Not at this time, I'm afraid," he replies. "Have you anything for me?"

"Oh, I couldn't impose. I haven't published a thing yet."

Which is true enough when it comes to a "Lucy Strong" by-line.

Hiedler smiles at me. "I'm imposing on you, Fraulein Strong. Please allow me to return the favour."

"Yes, but you're a *real* writer."

"Please," he says, "Herr Christoph has spoken so highly of your work. I insist that you allow me to read it."

"Well, if you'd be so kind, I should be enormously grateful."

It's tricky, exchanging highly confidential information under the eyes of strangers in a packed quasi-public space. But my information is buried in a pulp story, and the story is sealed in a Manila envelope.

Hiedler accepts the envelope with a gracious smile and another overstated bow. "Vielen Dank, Fraulein Strong."

We both know it might be suspicious to leave at this point. He resumes his seat, and we make idle conversation, abetted in no small part by the artless chatterbox from Christopher's shared flat. Only when I finish my glass of red wine and Hiedler empties his soda water do I make my farewells.

Hiedler rises from his seat. "The Schöneberg district is notoriously dissolute, and night has fallen. I shall accompany you both to your destinations."

The Schöneberg district is the part of Berlin with the largest population of homosexuals. Though rough and run-down, it's probably the safest neighbourhood in Berlin for a woman walking alone. Even if it weren't, I'm rather a difficult woman to harm.

I smile at Hiedler and politely decline. "I live close by," I add, without giving details. "I'll be fine."

Refilling her glass from my bottle, Sally doesn't bother to look up. "I'm meeting my new man here at eight."

As I make my way up Motzstrasse towards the Nollendorfplatz, I realise I'm being followed. Smiling at the irony, I turn into the darkness of a narrow alley, which a law-abiding soul in Berlin would avoid as a reeking obstacle course of prostitutes and punters, dope fiends, muggers, rapists, murderers, and lust-murderers.

The man follows me. He's too tall to be Hiedler, or anyone else from my tiny new circle of Berlin acquaintances. It appears my cover is blown.

So quickly! How?

Is Hiedler's cover blown, as well?

Is Christopher's?

Or has one of them betrayed me?

Bypassing a couple copulating against a grimy wall, I approach the busy Kleiststrasse. I can lose my tail in the popular Kleist Casino, or slip into the Verona-Lounge. The Lesbian bar won't admit an unaccompanied male.

The uncertain starlight in the narrow byway is more than sufficient for my inhuman eyes, and a backward glance catches my tail rounding a bend in the alley. He's a tall, bony, elderly German with a bright potato nose and a Father Christmas beard. He uses an Alpenstock as a walking-stick but has a spry gait. He's too far away for me to catch his scent.

If the old man works for the German puppet government, we're essentially both agents of SIS. However, I can't assume he does. Occupied territories and independent nations alike resent the acquisitiveness and alien technology of my homeland, which has conquered much of the world and contends with China and the United States for the rest. Many of these powers play in Berlin.

As I gain the neon-bright Kleiststrasse, I discover the Bohemian boulevard is being monitored by a tripod, its underside enameled blue, red, and white.

The British Empire's three-legged battle-machines are taller than a three-story house and built with technology reverse-engineered from the failed "Martian" invasion of '02. The tripods tend to discourage approach, especially when the agile tentacles are lowered, as they are in this case.

I turn towards the tripod, and the man drops back, but he remains on my tail with the tenacity of a tick. I'll mention him to the woman at the door of the Verona-Lounge. She knows me, and she will make his life much too interesting to worry about me.

The fighting-machine's three legs remain as motionless as tree-trunks while I pass, but one of the tentacles which dangle like clustered vines gives a twitch. Then it strikes with a serpentine speed no mortal could avoid. On the busy street, I must allow it to wrap around my torso and raise me into the air.

It carries me through the open hatch into the cockpit, where a fair-haired young lieutenant of the Royal Tripod Corps sits at the controls. His eyes are slate and his shave is so close his pores should be bleeding. He smiles at me in no friendly fashion.

"What ho, Fraulein! Sprechen Sie Englisch?" The pilot speaks in a toffee-nosed accent. "You're pale enough for a Boche," he continues in our native language, with a laugh like tearing burlap. "But you jolly well look like a Gipsy."

"I'm English!" I assure him, shaking in every limb.

"I've a ripping advantage up here, Fraulein. I saw you leaving that pervert club only moments before a known agitator," he says. "I've had quite enough of you rummy sorts selling British secrets to German subversives."

"You've made a mistake, sir." My voice quavers with the terror of an innocent woman. My arms aren't bound by the metal "rope" in a way which prevents me opening my portfolio, so I withdraw the government-issued identification papers of my alias. "I don't know any subversives," I assure the pilot. "I'm a British citizen, loyal to king and country."

"What utter rot." He laughs. "I'm sure you were meeting with that Hiedler blighter. Don't try to deny it, I know what he looks like. Can't stop talking the Empire down, that one. I ought to take you to my superiors."

Hiedler is a British intelligence agent. His overt talk against "English oppressors" makes him a valuable operative for the Empire, which has no idea he's a double agent. But there's no use blowing his cover by telling the tripod pilot that. Especially when the pilot's nothing more than a bloody fool acting on his own initiative. Britain has many secret agents in the tripod corps, but a Secret Intelligence Service operative would never be so stupid as to sweep up a suspected spy with a tripod—especially on one of the busiest streets in Berlin.

"Sir," I say, voice rising, "I don't know anyone named Adler. Is he German? I don't even speak German!"

"You don't, eh?" The pilot strokes the point of his chin, as if considering. "Well, I might be able to let you go. If you demonstrate your loyalty."

I've heard of this sort of thing, though I've never witnessed it, or personally known anyone who's admitted to experiencing it. It's rumoured to happen to Irish girls, Kikuyu girls, Maori girls, red Indian girls, black Indian girls, German girls—everyone except English girls.

My looks bring me many sorts of attention which many other Englishwomen fail to receive.

"How can I prove my loyalty to England, sir?" I ask, trembling in voice and limbs.

"Why, I'll show you." The pilot smiles like a wolf spotting a fallen lamb. "I'll show you precisely what you need to do."

Starting towards me, he reaches for the buttons of his trousers.

"You daft monster." Now there's not a bit of panic in my voice. Only ice. "You've taken your last victim."

My captor laughs as if I'm more amusing than Chaplin's tramp. He's not much older than Christopher's singer friend. He's probably got a girl at home, or a boy, and a loving family, and none with any true notion of what business their proud soldier lad gets up to in uniform.

I don't have all my true father's abilities. I can't seize the human will by meeting someone's eyes. I don't need to. This fool approaches me as willingly as a pup its dam.

"No need to fuss," he says. "You'll love it, once you've had a taste." His smile fades as he looks more closely at my carefully made-up face. "Why, you're a bally old bint. Didn't realise. But you're Rubenesque. That's all right, isn't it."

His hand fastens on my shoulder like a bulldog's jaws.

I spread my arms, loosening the tentacle like an unsecured rope. The pilot stares, stunned by a feat mortals think impossible. The overlapping rings of tripod tentacles are made of the "Martian" aluminium alloy, which is tough enough to resist even supernatural strength. However, the alloy is expensive and difficult to make, so the interior parts of the tentacles are brass and steel and rubber.

I slap a silencing palm over the pilot's mouth, tightening fingers and thumb on his jaws like a bench vice. Then, with a quickness unknown to mortals, I use my left hand to tear his arms off. The heated iron and salt scent of blood fills the space as deliciously as pine smoke.

I shouldn't. There are SIS regulations. There are laws. Until now, in situations involving British service personnel, I haven't. I thought I never would.

But I'm extraordinarily provoked. And his sort don't do this sort of thing only the one time. They especially don't do it with enough confidence to leave the hatch open unless they've been at it a while. I won't leave him free to prey again, here or anywhere; and I don't see that the authorities will agree he deserves prosecution.

So, before the pilot's barely begun to bleed, I've pulled off his white silk scarf and bent his head sideways. He's gone into shock and offers no more resistance than fog. I open my mouth and my canine teeth slide to their full length as I lower my head.

I drink until his heartbeat fails.

Discarding his corpse, I peel the tentacle from my body like the coils of a dead boa. I pound my fists on the instrument panel as if playing a carillon keyboard, but I strike hard enough to cause damage. As a tripod pilot, I know better ways to disable the fighting-machines, but I want to suggest the activity of German radicals.

When I've crippled the tripod, I surveille its surroundings through the windscreen. I spot Dolf Hiedler on the brightly lit pavement of the Kleiststrasse, walking with his portfolio. Then a mechanical lunges from a dark alley-mouth to seize him.

Have you heard about the golden woman?

Though Dr Krüger's Maschinenmenschen sometimes figure in scientific romances and improbable French post-cards, his creations offer only rudimentary improvements on traditional automata. They're powered by batteries, and they're responsive to a narrow range of voice commands, which mostly involve shooting or seizing people. Otherwise, his mechanical men are as limited as a clockwork mouse, and not nearly as comely.

The mechanical woman seizing Hiedler resembles no automaton I've seen. She has the yellow-white sheen of the alien alloy and the geometric design of an Arts Décoratifs statue. She moves with the speed and grace of a gazelle. She is beautiful.

"She cannot exist," I whisper.

The pedestrians haven't time to register the automaton's appearance before she's popped Hiedler's head off his shoulders like a pippin off its stem. His eyes bulge like boiled eggs. Perhaps he sees his neck stump fountaining blood to a height of several inches before the golden woman pitches his head away like a cricket ball. It strikes no one before it comes to rest in the street, but some onlookers scream. This is too *Grand Guignol* even for jaded Berliners.

The golden woman discards Hiedler's body like an empty potato sack, then disappears into the alley with the portfolio containing the typescript I gave Hiedler.

My story is coded with the secrets of the British space programme.

I lunge for the open hatch but pull myself up short.

"You can't catch the golden woman," I remind myself. "You've no idea where she's bound, and you couldn't track her in this stinking city even if the alloy had a scent."

I shove my identity papers into my portfolio. Withdrawing a handkerchief, I use it to wipe every surface I might have touched, then mop my skin and sop my coat where the blood of dismemberment sprayed. I sling the portfolio over my shoulder, then peer through the hatch at the base of the cowl.

I don't see, scent, or hear anyone close by. It appears the old German who was following me has quit the scene. No fool he, then.

"Miss Harker."

The German steps from beneath the balcony shadowing the stairwell of a closed cellar-shop. He's too far away to be heard by human ears. His quiet words strike mine like a shout.

"Miss Harker—" he's speaking English "—do not linger in the tripod."

The old man's disguised his voice. He's changed his looks enough to trick even my eyes. I cannot catch his scent from three stories above. I don't need to. I knew whom he was when he spoke my name.

His presence is an extraordinarily dangerous development.

Does he suspect I no longer serve the British Empire?

"A new make of analytical engine has automated wireless transmitter-receivers," he softly remarks. "If this tripod has such an engine, it's reporting it's been vandalised."

A look about finds no one else nearby. Those at a distance ignore the fighting-machine as if it were empty pavement. None of this is surprising; no one wants to attract the notice of a tripod.

I take off my shoes and call, "Descending."

Grasping the implications for my modesty, the old man turns away. I leap through the hatchway. Holding my footgear in one hand makes jumping from a three-story height more awkward, but I alight on the pavement like a mortal who's skipped a couple of steps.

As I slip on my pumps, I tell him, "I've already heard the rumour about two-way wireless in tripods, and already noticed this one has a wireless aerial of unusual design. Shall we go?"

"It's no rumour," my step-uncle says, falling in beside me. "I have the information from my brother."

We walk away from the fighting-machine with the unhurried steps of the blameless. I peel off my overcoat and discard it in a rubbish bin. Nothing ties the bloody garment to me, and pilot's salt is popular here. I look like just another overheated addict discarding her attire in the middle of winter.

"I'm sorry he—" my uncle nods towards the tripod hood "—tried to compromise your virtue." He regards my flushed countenance. "But he's given you the opportunity to enjoy your favourite repast."

I don't bother to protest; on every point save my virtue, Sherlock Holmes is correct.

Berlin's night sky holds almost as many aëroplanes, airships, and wingless little eighth-ray flyers as the day. The closest aircraft is an Avro Avian 594 biplane bearing the R.A.F. roundel. The two-seater catches my eye by tipping its starboard wing down. The noise of propeller and petrol engine and the hum of bracing wires become louder as the aëroplane sinks closer. The lone occupant turns a delicate, high-coloured face to observe us through aviator goggles before tilting the nose of the craft up. The 'plane rises like a kestrel for the *Victoria*.

My uncle looks at me. "That was your friend, Miss Stein."

"We rarely know each other's assignments, but I'm not surprised M's also sent her here for the king's visit."

"M has sent so many of us to Berlin," says Holmes, and I can only hope there is no other reason for his presence here—and remain entirely on my guard in his presence.

"I—that green Opel is slowing down."

Holmes follows my gaze to the approaching motor-car. "That's not an aerial for listening to Funk-Stunde AG."

"Some unmarked police motor-cars in Berlin have two-way wireless. The apparatus must fill the back seat of this one."

The Opel beetles closer to the kerb amid a fanfare of angry horns, finally double-parking a few yards away. We proceed as if we have no reason to expect police attention.

The Opel's sole occupant unfolds a long frame from behind the wheel, revealing a fedora and trench coat and world-weary air. The gas street-lamps ensure a clear view of the man's dark hair, clean-shaven face, and prominent mole. I've never seen him before, but I recognise him from his British Intelligence dossier. He's Detective Inspector Rath, a compromised Berlin Homicide dick.

His eyes target us as unwaveringly as the Dreyse semi-automatic pistol in his fist.

"Hands in the air, terrorists."

Holmes and I comply, and an eighth-ray flyer with the R.A.F. roundel swoops down to carry us away.

I expect to be questioned within moments of setting foot on the flight deck of the *HMS Victoria*. However, it seems the security officers have more urgent concerns than a couple of suspected radicals. One barely glances at Holmes and me before ordering us to the brig under armed guard.

Our steps echo on iron bulkheads as two R.A.F. Police corporals conduct us down an empty flight of harshly illuminated metal stairs. At the bottom, one corporal undogs a weather-tight metal door while the other snaps several wall switches. The men escort us into a narrow, chilly passageway of iron surfaces and glaring bulbs, with a deckhead scarcely higher than our skulls.

Despite the ventilation fans, the air is stale and smells of emptiness. As a holiday get-away, the brig isn't much more appealing than the wind-swept open deck.

We pass a recessed area, which an American would call a kitchenette, and approach another door. This one is a grid of thick iron strips or flat bars, riveted where they cross. Beyond the grid, the passageway passes four closed cell doors of the same design, two on a side.

The passageway ends at a white-gold alloy door. It's solid, with a lock and a closed peephole hatch. The door isn't marked with the holy cross, but I wonder if it secures a compartment designed for the confinement and destruction of supernaturals. All British war-ships have such a cell, though typically it's not in the brig.

The policeman who looks Irish unlocks the passageway door and the closest cell. The other policeman, who looks Bengali, speaks in a Liverpool accent.

"Inside, you two."

Holmes and I comply. The cell is a barren little iron box, as likely to confine a supernatural as one made of cardboard. Our cuffs are steel and our captors never drew their service revolvers. They have no notion what I am.

As the Irishman locks our cell door, I hear the Scouser leave the brig, dogging the weather-tight door behind him. The Irishman locks the passageway door and disappears into the kitchenette.

Holmes and I move as far from our cell door as the tiny space allows. We've been frisked and disarmed; my portfolio and his walking-stick were also taken. Our hands are cuffed behind our backs.

"Miss Harker," Holmes murmurs, "I've deduced you wouldn't appreciate it if I removed my disguise and informed our captors they've made a mistake."

My stomach contracts as if filled suddenly with ice-water, but I answer with the calm of a loyal SIS agent. "My mission wouldn't benefit from exposure of my identity. And there's another consideration."

"What is that?"

"From the tripod," I say, "I saw another British agent, an Austrian called Dolf Hiedler. As I watched, he was killed in the street by a golden mechanical woman."

Holmes raises his powder-whitened brows in a rare display of surprise. "A golden mechanical woman, did you say?"

"The mechanical had a feminine shape and the visible portions were made of the alien alloy," I said. "She—it killed the man and appropriated his portfolio, which holds information intended for SIS. Then the mechanical fled into an alley. I saw no one giving the mechanical orders, but my view was obstructed."

"Dr Krüger's machine-men aren't capable of independent action," Holmes says.

"The design of the golden woman was far more advanced than Krüger's ambulatory tins. And far more aesthetically pleasing."

"A novel design." The shaggy brows draw together in thought. "Did you observe a wireless aerial on the device?"

"I saw none."

After a moment, my uncle says, "Last night, I overheard three Ring-brothers discussing a 'goldener Maschinen-mädchen.'"

"The gangsters saw her?"

Holmes shakes his head. "They were sharing rumours that a 'golden machine-maiden' has been glimpsed several times in Berlin over the last week. The Ring-brothers concluded this mechanical must be some British device or scheme, if it exists at all."

"Only Britain possesses the secret of the alien alloy," I say slowly. "But I've heard nothing from SIS about a new automaton design."

"Nor have I, but that means little," he says.

"Indeed. M would inform neither of us of a new automaton unless he deemed it necessary."

M is his brother and my stepfather, Mycroft Holmes. M is his code name as Director of SIS.

"Whatever the Maschinenmädchen's provenance," I continue, "Hiedler was serving British interests. It's essential I recover his portfolio."

My uncle's lips curve in the false beard. "I share your disinclination to remain in durance vile."

"I'll minimise noise," I say, "but someone just might suspect a supernatural's aboard the *Victoria* once I tear a few doors off their hinges."

"We cannot all be so subtle, but I have an alternative plan I hope you'll find acceptable."

Holmes pulls the skirts of his greatcoat behind his back for a few moments. When the skirts settle back in place, concentration tenses his facial muscles. I hear a gentle click. A second click, and Holmes brings his hands into view.

Like a double-headed baby snake, a chain with opened hand-cuffs coils on one palm. The other displays the pair of small lock-picking tools he's withdrawn from his greatcoat hem. I return my uncle's smile, then turn to offer him my locked cuffs.

He's just unlocked the passageway door when the corporal sticks his head round the corner for a look.

"Bloody hell!"

Though young and quick, he's not finished unfastening his holster before my left fist sinks into his gut. As he folds with an explosion of breath, my right fist meets his chin. I catch the man as he goes limp and waltz him into the cell. Holmes follows, closing the doors to suggest they're locked.

I confirm that the corporal's Enfield revolver is loaded, then hand it to Holmes. As he examines the weapon, lingering over the novelty of a safety on a revolver, I remove the corporal's Sam Browne belt. When I begin divesting the man of his greatcoat, my uncle grasps my intention and turns his back to give me privacy.

With volunteer-nurse efficiency, I strip the corporal to his under layers. Then I cuff his arms behind his back and cocoon him in his greatcoat.

Though the shoes prove too small, the peaked cap fits snugly. The uniform is tight across my chest and hips, but the legs and sleeves are a bit too long. No member of the Women's R.A.F. wears this uniform, and no one in the R.A.F. wears pumps with Cuban heels on duty, but perhaps from a distance I'll look the part.

"Ready, uncle?"

Holmes turns about, extending the revolver grip first. "My eyes were never as keen as a blood-drinker's."

We're approaching the weather-tight door when its valve wheel turns. I gesture for Holmes to retreat and begin backing up, revolver pointed at the door. It swings heavily open, revealing two figures.

I recognise them and know that Christopher and I have been compromised.

Sally Bolle greets my levelled weapon with a laugh. "I was warned you might break gaol, sweet."

There's a black leather page-boy's cap on her Louise Brooks bob. Her sleeveless black leather body-suit is buckled at the throat and girt by a gun-belt with an empty holster. She completes the look with calf-length heeled boots of black leather. I'd find the ensemble quite stirring, were it worn by a different woman.

She holds a key-ring in one hand; the other points a Ruby pistol at my heart. The keys jingle as she indicates her gleaming metal companion.

"You might kill me, Miss Strong," Sally says, "but you can't kill the machine maiden. You will put your weapon on the floor and the pair of you will put your hands in the air."

I place the revolver on the deck-plate as carefully as a full tea-cup, then join Holmes in elevating my hands. Sally takes a quick look round, as if searching for a guard.

Returning her gaze to us, she says, "Maria."

Though the golden machine-woman has received no command, she picks up the discarded Enfield by the barrel, then hands it to Sally. As the mortal slips the revolver in her gun-belt, Maria lays one alloy hand on the back of my neck and the other on the back of Holmes's neck. I remember how easily she decapitated Hiedler.

Mechanicals do not speak.

"Sir and miss," she says in German, "don't try to escape. Otherwise, I must kill you."

She has a soft voice, light and lovely as a lark's, with the same surprising suggestion of melancholy.

At her death threat, Sally shows Holmes and me a smile which makes Maria's icy hand seem as warm as the Tenerife sun. "Believe Maria, my sweets," she says in English, "or you won't live to see the stars."

A twitch of Sally's pistol directs Holmes and me out of the brig. Maria follows, keeping her hands cupped on our necks.

The propeller drone is louder in the stair-well. There is no one on the stairs or in the open hatchway at the top. The opening frames a cloudy sky, with stars peering through a rift like firelit cats' eyes.

Sally says, "Up we go, sweets."

As we start up the stairs, a shadow blocks the stars, then descends in a blur of motion. A leather-gloved hand snatches the Ruby from Sally's grip and presses the muzzle into the soft flesh beneath her chin, tilting her head up.

The golden woman releases Holmes and me and raises her hands in the air.

The newcomer is a slim figure in black pilot's leathers. The coat hangs open, revealing W.R.A.F. wings on the left breast of the officer's tunic. With her free hand, the pilot pushes her goggles up over her leather flight helmet.

Meeting Sally's glare, she says, "No sudden moves."

I wonder if Sally will lash out in envy. With four syllables, the newcomer has revealed a far superior voice. Low and rich, clear and dark, it's smoke diamond to the cabaret singer's brittle sugar glass.

I smile at the pilot.

For a second, she holds my gaze. Her eyes are dark and keen with intelligence, her features fine and merciless as a rapier. The pilot's cap covers her hair, but the stray lock on her brow is a curve of dark bronze limned with gold. Her slight build suggests youth and weakness. Her rosy complexion and fur-lined coat suggest a marked sensitivity to the cold German night.

Clarimal Stein is centuries old and as indifferent to extremes of weather as a mountain. Her strength can match a werewolf's. Her bright colour indicates she has recently drunk deeply of blood. She is an upiór—the vampire once named Mircalla, Countess Karstein, better known to history as Carmilla.

Her nostrils flare as she studies my companions. Her gaze lingers briefly on the mechanical woman. When she takes a second look at my uncle, I realise she's recognised his scent through a lingering odour of tobacco smoke.

She extends her empty left hand and addresses Sally with a high-blooded Austrian accent. "The keys."

"Bloody Ösi spy." Scowling, Sally lets the key-ring fall on Clarimal's palm. "You won't get far."

"I know the woman as Sally Bolle," I tell Clarimal. "Her mechanical is called Maria. Maria speaks German."

Clarimal's eyes widen slightly, and her next words are in German. "Maria and Fraulein Bolle shall enjoy the hospitality of the brig while I notify the R.A.F.P. of their presence on the *Victoria*."

Sally says, "My presence here is authorised—"

"The senior officer on duty will determine that," Clarimal says. "You and Maria will lie on the cell floor."

Once they've complied, Clarimal passes the Ruby pistol to Holmes, then uses an abandoned cuff to shackle the pair together, wrist to wrist, with the chain looped like a flapper's pearls around one of the bars. I aim the recovered revolver at the mechanical's eye. My experiences with Dr Krüger's primitive machine-men suggest a bullet through her glass eye won't find a vital centre, but Maria complies as if it would.

What does it mean, a mechanical behaving as if she can think?

Clarimal locks the cell door; then the three of us stand so the prisoners cannot read our lips.

"The machine-woman will free them soon," Clarimal says quietly in English. "It's fortunate my biplane is nearby."

"I'll swing the propeller, but three's a crowd, when you've only two seats," I say. "Miss Stein, if you would take my uncle off the *Victoria*, I'll wire a warning to Christopher Isherwood that his cover may have been compromised. Then I'll recover the papers which the golden woman stole from a British agent."

"I'll hand-prop," says Carmilla. "Look for the papers."

Though she's not part of it, she knows about my mission to pass British spaceship technology to the Americans. It was supposed to be our last action against Britain before we disappeared from the face of the earth.

Holmes regards us with lifted brows. "If Britain has the papers, why take them?"

I answer. "It's intelligence intended for SIS eyes only."

Clarimal hands me Sally's key-ring. "I'll wire Isherwood before Mr Holmes and I leave the *Victoria*," she says. "Where do I reach Isherwood?"

I give her the particulars.

"Miss Stein," I say, "one final matter."

Though my uncle's looking on, I sweep her into my arms.

After a moment's surprise, my mate tilts her face up. Her eyes meet mine, intent, asking. Holding her gaze, I lower my head. Her breath brushes my lips, intimate as a whisper. Then her arms slip around me, pulling me against her. A mortal's spine would snap under the force of our embrace as we exchange what might prove our last kiss.

We've never told my uncle we're more than friends. But we've never needed to, have we? He's Sherlock Holmes.

As Clarimal and I step apart, I brace myself for his disapproving stare.

Holmes says, "Thank you for your trust."

Lest his words undo me, I turn away, indicating the door at the end of the passageway. "If that's not a security office, I'll seek the papers elsewhere. Once I'm off the *Victoria*, I'll wire Miss Stein at the Lehrter Bahnhof."

Clarimal won't be leaving Berlin. Her dirt-lined coffin is here with her renfield. Clarimal must be in her coffin by dawn or suffer the torments of Hell.

"We'll await your word," she tells me, and leaves the brig with Holmes.

As I approach the alloy door, random notes of a low, intense male voice pipe blurrily through the closed peephole cover. Keeping to one side, I slide the little trap door back slowly, lest it make some sound which must betray my presence as surely as the cocking of a revolver. My action exposes an unglazed eyehole which emits bright electric light and the scents of two male mortals. One scent I recognise.

The opening reveals a laboratory. The far wall has a second alloy door with a dark peephole. Instead of a porthole, the bulkhead to the right has a square, openable window of the sort seen in the luxury class of steamships.

The laboratory holds stainless steel tables and shelves with a curious array of scientific instruments and workmen's and jeweller's tools. Electrodes and Bunsen burners and Tesla coils mingle with spanners and loupes, cogs and wheels, hammers and welding torches.

In an open area, two mortals stand, facing one another with the air of rival tomcats.

I haven't seen the infamous Herr Doktor Krüger since the Great War, when the false report of the German scientist's death was celebrated across the world. He's approaching ninety, but seems hardly to have aged in the nearly fifteen years since he turned his coat to serve Britain. A scrawny figure with an oversized head and bald pate, he's as timeless as a petrified tree, and he still wears wire spectacles with thick round lenses which might suit a myopic owl. He's aiming an alloy handgun of an unfamiliar, fluted design at the mortal facing him.

The stranger may be as old as Krüger, but he appears more youthful and more attractive, if you ignore an intensity of glare which suggests a tenuous acquaintance with sanity. His pale mane is tousled, his eye shadowed by a heavy brow. I think he's an eccentric wearing one black glove until he gestures dismissively at Krüger. His right hand is a sophisticated prosthetic not dissimilar to Maria's hands.

Krüger addresses him in German. "If you don't cooperate, Herr Rotwang, you will regret it." He jabs his peculiar pistol at the other man. "A pile of ashes is easy to dispose of. And who will be surprised to hear an absent-minded neurotic like you opened the window to star-gaze and fell out?"

"I don't care what you want. I don't care what the British want." The stranger crosses his arms over his chest. "I'm not sharing the secret of my androids with anyone."

Krüger glances around the laboratory, and I lean away from the peephole.

Pain sears the side of my head, and I hear the flat crack of a gunshot and whine of a ricochet. Caught off balance, I fall. The keys drop, jingling on the iron deckplate as I catch myself on my hands and knees.

With her left hand, the golden woman snaps the chain cuffing her to Sally Bolle, as if eager to put distance between them. With her right hand, Maria fits her Mauser pistol inside her open belly. Then she touches the place where a mortal's breastbone would be, and the clam-shell doors of her abdomen swing silently shut.

I've dealt with automata for some fifteen years and never thought of hiding a weapon inside one.

Rising, I reel like a drunk dancing her first Charleston. My skull and ears are ringing. Blood flows down the side of my head and perfumes the air. My fingertip finds a raw groove across my temple.

With a screech of iron, Maria rips the locked door open. As she steps from the cell, I seize her wrists. My strength exceeds that of any conventional mechanical, yet Maria frees her arms as easily as I'd pull mine from a mortal's grip.

Her elbow strikes my breastbone like a pile driver. Knocked backwards, I strike my skull on the iron bulkhead and hear the celery crunch of snapping bone. I sink down, lights filling my vision like the birth of a galaxy.

The stars fade to reveal the golden woman's face close to mine. She speaks through the slit of her moveless metal mouth, too softly for Sally's mortal ears.

"Es tut mir leid."

It gives me sorrow, she says.

I'm sorry.

She moves carefully as she raises me, but the pain in my head spins like a cyclone, obliterating everything.

I'm in London, between missions, and my mother has invited me to afternoon tea. She has no idea I've become a double agent, and good reason to suppose I'm friendly with a vampire. She's a fellow SIS intelligence operative and England's greatest vampire slayer.

Altogether, I anticipate an excruciating visit.

There's little enough to eat or drink in London, with the Great War raging. But a few tea sandwiches await our attention, and her old silver tea-pot exhales the floral fragrance of Darjeeling.

My mother dismisses the parlour-maid and pours for us both. Like a young mother cat, I watch with a wariness I cannot quite hide. I expect she's no less cautious, but when she lowers the tea-pot, Wilhelmina Murray Harker Holmes smiles at me.

"My dear Lucy," she says, "you mustn't blame yourself for telling me something I should have realised long before."

She doesn't explain what she means. She doesn't need to.

On the Hollow Earth mission, I informed her that vampires aren't emotionless killing machines. I didn't stop to think how learning the falsity of this widely-held view—one she shared—must make her feel. Before I was born, her closest friend was slain upon being turned, out of fear of what she must become.

"Mother," I say, "I can only regret my thoughtlessness—"

"Never apologise for telling me the truth."

We sip tea. She nibbles on a cucumber sandwich, and I'm rather less delicate with the roast beef and horseradish. I take a longer drink and start to relax.

"The next time we have tea," she says, "I hope Miss Stein will join us."

I nearly spray my mother with hot liquid.

She smiles gently.

"I've realised you would have destroyed the Countess Karnstein long ago, if she were a threat to mortals," she says. "I know she can drink tea. And—" She pauses, her expression sobering. "I should like to make amends for my—previous conduct."

She refers to her attempt to destroy Clarimal Stein during our Hollow Earth mission.

"I know she must be wary of me," my mother says. "For many reasons."

For many reasons?

My mind fills with memories of last night and Clarimal. I hope my ruddy countenance obscures my flush. I shouldn't like my mother thinking of me in bed with a man, either, but that she would understand.

"If Miss Stein isn't interested in joining us, I will understand," my mother continues. "But, whatever her feelings towards me, I'm glad you have a friend who understands you."

I cannot quite suppress my surprise as I say, "Thank you."

"It couldn't have been easy for you, growing up a dhampir among mortals. You were tasked to protect them, yet craved their blood."

I realise she doesn't suspect the true nature of my relationship with Clarimal and suppress a sigh of relief. My mother already blames herself for what Dracula did to her, and the sight of me is a constant reminder of that. I've no wish to start her blaming herself for something else she never caused.

I hide my thoughts with a smile. "Mother, please be assured you supervised your blood-thirsty little monster quite adequately."

"Never a monster, Lucy."

I was joking, and yet my mother's words make my throat tighten.

"Only dreadfully isolated," she says, "as the only one of your kind known to exist."

She takes a sip of her tea.

"I know your life makes it difficult," she says. "But I've always wanted you to find someone who makes you as happy as Mr Holmes makes me."

I've never much liked Mycroft Holmes, but even if I were wild with enthusiasm for their match, it wouldn't inspire me to want a husband.

I clear my throat. "Mother, I may yet find a man I'd care to spend my—his—his life with—"

"I thought your father might always be alone."

She doesn't call M my father, and she doesn't mean Dracula. She is referring to her former husband and my legal father, Jonathan Harker. He has always treated me like his daughter, though he knows I'm no more kin of his than a bat.

"His experiences in Transylvania scarred him," my mother continues. "And I didn't quite realise what they were, until he told me recently."

I've long since deduced that Dracula's "brides" preyed on Jonathan Harker in ways which didn't stop with taking his blood. "Mother, you don't need to tell m—"

"If I might finish?"

I force silence round myself like an iron band.

"You know Stoker's record of events is…at great variance in many ways with the truth," my mother says. "But neither is it true, what the rumour mill says about Miss Westenra and me—"

"Mother!" Her indifference to female charms is as clear to my inhuman senses as a new window-pane. "I know you would never—"

"Many girls at our school did such things with one another willingly," she says. "But your father didn't want any of the things Dracula did to him."

—the things Dracula did to him—

The blood rushes from my head until I fear I'll discover what mortals mean when they say they "swooned." Through the sudden roaring in my ears, I hear my mother speak again. "I'm glad Jonathan was able to find happiness with another woman."

"Ah," I say faintly. "Right. Of course."

As a child, I had craved their reunion with the selfish intensity of a tidal wave.

To my surprise, she lays her hand on mine.

"If you've found someone who makes you happy, Lucy, I shan't cavil over mortal or vampire, man or woman."

Before I can begin to think of a response, Maria's voice interrupts.

"Fraulein Harker, sind Sie am Leben?"

My mother disappears. The town house she shares with Mycroft Holmes dissipates like mist, taking my memory-dream with it.

"Sie sind nicht tot," the golden woman says, as my eyes slit open. "Können Sie gehen?"

You aren't dead. Can you walk?

Maria's holding me upright and studying my face. Her fingers grip my upper arms firmly, but without pain. My head throbs like a kettledrum beneath a berserker's mallets. My weapon and gun-belt are gone, my hands cuffed behind my back. A cold wind blows steadily into my face.

We're on the flight deck. No one else is visible in the blaze of the electric lights. Cloud covers the sky like a rumpled blanket. The wind of passage shreds the white cloud of my breath and flutters my hair and garments like pennons.

Aft, aëroplanes are tied down on either side of the electrically-illuminated run-way. The nearest, an Avro Avian 594 biplane, wears the R.A.F. roundel like an heraldic device. The W.R.A.F. uses the 594 as a messenger 'plane, and Clarimal is serving SIS under cover as a messenger. If that's Clarimal's aircraft, she and my uncle are still on the *Victoria*.

Have they been apprehended?

I meet the golden woman's glass gaze and answer in German. "I can walk."

"I'll let you go," she says. "If you don't try to escape, I won't kill you."

"I won't try to escape," I tell her, and I won't. Despite the claims of sensational fiction, blood-drinkers cannot outrun a bullet.

Maria releases me, keeping one hand near my shoulder, to catch me if I sway or attempt to bolt. Her other hand produces the machine pistol, which she points at my skull. She moves almost as quickly as I would, were I uninjured.

Es tut mir leid.

Maria apologised to me.

A mechanical apologised to me.

Chose to apologise to me.

She says, "We're going to the island."

She gestures with her Mauser at the super-structure, which is forward of our location on the starboard side of the *Victoria*. The island rises seven stories above the flight deck and houses navigation, communications, the bridge, and other critical functions of the air-borne aircraft carrier. The top story is a small glass-walled cabin, used for observation and air traffic control.

One of the rooftop aerials is an upright, concave rectangular grid, which turns in circles like a kinetic abstract sculpture. It's the first radiolocation aerial in use, but won't be the last. It's more reliable than watching the night sky with binoculars and search-lights while hoping you find an obstacle before it finds you.

I speak in German. "I'm surprised to be alive."

Though I haven't said her name or asked a question, Maria responds. "Fraulein Bolle thought she killed you, because your head was so bloody. She told me to take your body to the island and left the brig, but you were alive, so I waited for your death. After a while, your heartbeat grew stronger, so I realised you wouldn't die."

I have a strong thirst and a dehydration headache, and the pain of gunshot wound and cracked skull is gone. I've healed without drinking blood, which requires more time. I've been unconscious for at least a couple of hours.

I address the mechanical in English. "Miss Bolle didn't tell you to make sure I was dead?"

For a moment, Maria regards me in silence, and I suppose she doesn't understand the language. Then she responds in English. "Miss Bolle said the British don't care if you're alive or dead."

I think of Maria separating Hiedler's head from his shoulders as easily as a child flicks a dandelion from its stem, but I utter the unwise words. "I've seen you kill."

"I don't like to kill, but must when they order me to," she says. "We must go to the island, Miss Harker."

I move slowly, as if gravely injured, but Maria makes no objection. Which confirms it. She wants to talk to me.

Like conversation, like apologies, volition is no trait of mechanicals. Their clockwork and electrodes dictate their tiny range of actions, until a part or battery fails. That is all.

"Maria," I say, "how came you to be?"

"Mr Rotwang made me." As if anticipating my next question, she says, "I don't know how. I only know that I woke up for the first time and he was facing me. I didn't know whom he was then, or what he'd done. I didn't know whom I was. I knew only how to move and how to speak German and English."

I risk a glance over my shoulder. "Who is Mr Rotwang?"

"The scientist who created me," says Maria, "and taught me about the world. After a few weeks, he said he lost the woman he loved, to death—he explained what death was, then, but he never explained what love was."

We reach the island, and I sag against the alloy exterior like a dizzy dipsomaniac. Maria keeps her pistol trained on me, but makes no attempt to chivvy me into motion.

Some distance forward of the island is an elevated platform for mooring eighth-ray flyers. There are aëroplanes parked beneath the platform, and a uniformed figure moving among them. He's too distant to hear us over the carrier propellers. It's possible he doesn't see us.

I look at Maria. "Why did Mr Rotwang mention his lost love?"

"He said he created me to look like her."

However beautiful and sophisticated, a mechanical cannot be mistaken for a real woman, but I say nothing.

"He said he loved me," Maria continues. "He started breathing like a man who'd been running, though he hadn't been running, and he started touching me. It was strange. I didn't like it."

I find myself speaking furiously, as if she were alive: "You don't need to put up with that."

"Mr Rotwang created me," Maria says, "as God created you. I won't cease functioning for centuries, Mr Rotwang says, unless someone destroys my electrodes or removes my atomic heart. He said he'd remove mine if I kept objecting when he touched me, so I didn't say anything else. I don't have a soul, so I cannot go to Heaven or Hell, as a person would. And I like being functional."

"You needn't cease functioning to leave Berlin or Rotwang."

"I have nowhere else to go."

I face her directly. "There's a whole wide world out there," I say. "You can avoid humans."

"Then I would be alone," Maria says. "Other machine-men are like automobiles. They don't talk. They don't notice me. They cannot."

I find myself sympathising with her.

She seems so alive!

From vampires and animals and Frankenstein's creation, we know that life can exist in flesh and blood even in the absence of a soul. But can life be kindled in something, however clever, created by man from mineral?

"Maria, is it possible there are other machine women or men made by Herr Rotwang?"

"He told me I am unique—"

The island door opens long enough to admit a familiar figure onto the brightly lit deck.

Sherlock Holmes is restored to his Alpenstock. His grease-paint and false beard and nose are gone, revealing the famous features. The decades have weathered his countenance, but there's hardly a seam in the pale skin.

He surveys the deck. When he sees me at gunpoint, his expression alters no more than a stone's. I don't need his deductive genius to recognise a bad omen.

"Our friend was helping you leave the *Victoria*," I call over the propeller racket. "Where has she gone?"

"She left me on the ground floor of the island," Holmes says. "I haven't seen her since."

Holmes and Clarimal should be long gone from the carrier. And would Holmes discard his disguise if he hadn't betrayed her?

"Uncle," I say, "if you would arrange for my release—"

"That's for Flight Lieutenant Wilk to decide."

"'Wilk'?" I say.

One of my step-brothers was christened John Hamish Adler Norton. As a spy in the Great War, he operated under the *nom de guerre* Auguste Lupa. Since then, he's used other fanciful aliases with imperial and lupine associations.

Wilk is the Polish word for wolf.

I say, "John's a bit out of his bailiwick." Indeed, he's almost four thousand miles from his base of operations in a Manhattan brownstone. "What's his full alias?"

Before Holmes can reply, a shout comes from the direction of the bow.

"Hoy!" The man from the flyer platform is approaching with the long-limbed stride and nervy energy of a greyhound. Under the R.A.F. Police cap, pale eyes linger on Maria as he aims his handgun and speaks in a Cardiff accent. "I don't recognise you lot."

Holmes says, "You don't recognise me?"

The corporal halts, squinting. His lips part. "Dear God," he says, "is it Mr Sherlock Holmes?"

He doesn't lower his Enfield revolver.

"Even if you be the detective himself," he says, "you've no business here—"

Behind Holmes, the door opens to reveal a flight lieutenant.

The corporal comes to attention. "Sir!"

"Corporal," says the officer plummily, "you've seen no one here, and any claim to the contrary will be dealt with severely."

He dismisses the corporal, who proceeds aft at a good clip, then turns to me. His expression alters, as if he's overturned a rock and found a squirming creature.

His dark hair is short, his shave fresh, and his scent *eau de bière blonde*. He has the roughening complexion of a mortal near forty, with a florid colour which clashes with the shirt showing like a urine stain in the V of his R.A.F. greatcoat. A gun-belt girds his substantial waist like a python, bearing a holstered Webley revolver.

Sherlock Holmes speaks. "Miss Harker, let me introduce you to Flight Lieutenant Adrian Wilk of the Royal Air Force Police Special Investigation Branch."

I smile at my step-brother with no warmth. "The pleasure is all his, I'm sure."

He's as corpulent as M and barely shorter than Holmes and me. He holds his broad shoulders back, with posture so erect, he might have a claymore up his arse. Yet he seems dwarfed by our uncle's austere frame.

He glances at my metal captor, then returns his half-lidded brown eyes to me.

"John," I say, "I've been mistakenly arrested—"

"Miss Harker, please," Wilk says. The plummy tones are gone, revealing an American accent almost aggressively plain. "Stop wasting our time and insulting our intelligence."

"Take your own advice," I say. "As head of British espionage operations in the United States, you know spies are occasionally snagged by their own side."

My candour about our intelligence roles causes neither Wilk nor Holmes to look at the golden woman. Perhaps they think she doesn't know English; but I suspect they believe she has the comprehension of a statue.

"Enough, Miss Harker," Wilk says. "You've already deduced we've discovered your treachery."

"Treachery?" I give him a disgusted look. "Sorry to dash the cup of joy from your lips, old boy, but I was under deep cover. And if you don't release me, this rummy rannygazoo will derail my mission and put other British operatives at risk."

Wilk shakes his massive head. "I warned my father not to trust females—especially when they're blood-suckers."

"Which pater did you warn?" I say. "Not Geoffrey Norton, I trust. Have you resumed the pretence that Uncle Sherlock is your father? Or do you mean M, who spawned you?"

My step-brother purses his lips, as if he's discovered a small dinosaur adorning his shoes with shit.

I turn to Holmes. "If you would warn your brother," I say. "M needs to pull other operatives from the field, lest they be harmed by Wilk's mistake."

Holmes considers for a moment, then looks at Wilk. "This is a singular situation, nephew, and not one in which we should act before every aspect has been understood. I've one or two matters I'd like to clear up, and you've said you need to secure an eighth-ray flyer. If you would give us a few minutes."

Dismissal by his idol heightens the glow of Wilk's complexion. But he's always wanted to replace Watson as Holmes's loyal assistant. Like a trained Alsatian wolf dog, he turns to the door.

"You might want to see how Herr Rotwang is faring," I tell him. "I witnessed Herr Doktor Krüger threatening him with a fancy new pistol he probably created in secret."

Holmes turns to me, brows rising, and I realise he had accepted the Empire's story of Krüger's death in the Great War. The golden woman makes a startled, almost animal sound, too soft for mortal ears. Wilk re-enters the island at an unwontedly brisk pace.

I call Wilk and his twin my "step-brothers" for lack of a better term. Mycroft Holmes has never scrupled to acknowledge his bastards (all of whom resulted from liaisons which occurred before he began courting my mother); but he's never acknowledged Wilk or his twin. This is because the affair occurred during a period of estrangement in the mother's marriage, and the boys received their legal father's name and affection.

The twins spent their childhood summers with us, as "distant Holmes cousins." I thought this explained the Holmes notes in their scents. Later, I would think coincidence explained the scent-notes which the twins shared with my first lover, Guiffrida Norton. My mother knew of my closeness with my school friend, and my stepfather deduced precisely how close we'd become. We never imagined our parents would withhold information so vital from us.

In Wilk's absence, Sherlock Holmes turns to me. "I must commend your caution, Miss Harker. You didn't use your personal typewriter."

This singular observation can mean only one thing. He's seen the story I gave Dolf Hiedler, and realised it's a coded message. Has he deciphered it?

I respond in an indifferent tone. "I've no idea why you're discussing typewriters, but you hardly need one to recognise my prose. There are decades' worth of examples in the sensational magazines."

"Your writing style confirms your treachery," Holmes says. "You and Miss Stein are double agents."

He *knows*.

I face my greatest challenge: persuading Sherlock Holmes he's made a mistake when he hasn't.

"I don't write about spies," I remind him, "and I cannot imagine how my fiction about vampires and man-wolves and extra-solar aliens would suggest a faltering in either my loyalty to Britain, or Miss Stein's." Hesitantly, I say, "Have you taken no royal bee jelly recently?"

I've impugned his mental acuity, but he replies imperturbably. "We've no direct evidence of wrong-doing on Miss Stein's part, though SIS have always kept a very close watch on her. But it was never difficult to imagine the former Countess Karnstein might turn against England. Few Austrians are fond of the country which has subjugated their native land."

I scowl. "This is your insight, after tutting my childhood self any number of times for jumping to conclusions?"

"By itself, Miss Stein's nationality means little," he replies. "But I've read the story you gave Hiedler, and I've discovered the secret code you buried in your pulp phantasy."

It was exceptionally well buried. The number of filler words between the code words varied, depending on the page.

"The only code I've dealt with lately," I lie, "is the one in the rant Hiedler shared with me."

"That message used a familiar SIS code," Holmes says. "It identified a minor double agent working against British interests—a pawn the United States can afford to sacrifice. But the code in your story, Miss Harker. You must have known I'd crack it."

Clarimal and I never supposed the cipher would baffle the scrutiny of Sherlock Holmes. We merely hoped he wouldn't see the coded information before we made our get-away.

I raise my eyebrows. "I can only ask what I said."

"Your message required you to use words not typically part of your style, and not quite right for your tale," Holmes says. "Such anomalies gave me the means to work backwards and uncover your hidden message—a message which reveals the secrets of our space programme. Secrets which, if betrayed, would destroy British dominance over the world."

He knows so much, I feel a terrible pressure to make a clean breast of it. I understand now why wrong-doers have confessed to him, when keeping silent would have preserved their liberty. But I'll not fold like a flannel and put Clarimal and Christopher at risk.

"Finally, I understand how you've gone so far astray," I tell my uncle. "You don't understand the alien technology any more than I do."

"Every 'backroom boy' of the spaceship project is enjoying the *Victoria*'s maiden cruise," he replies. "I've shared your decoded information with the Einsteins and the Curies. They confirm its accuracy."

I keep silent. There is no response whose falsity won't be obvious.

"Lucy," he says. "Everything is known." Sorrow suffuses his tone like nightfall. "How an Englishwoman could behave in such a manner is beyond my comprehension."

It happened almost fifteen years ago, but the memory remains as vivid as a fresh nightmare. The smell of gunsmoke. The raven-glossy hair tumbling loose as An falls, like a woman turned boneless. The flat sound of her body striking the stone floor, one arm caught beneath her. The skirt of her fur tunic brushing her exposed wrist as gently as a hummingbird's wing. M standing in Krüger's operating room, expressionless as a marble pillar. The Webley revolver smoking in M's hand as he confirms An is silenced permanently.

She was An of the Mezops, a Stone Age people of the Hollow Earth. Though England's interests were contrary to hers, she acted as my guide on a British intelligence mission.

Holmes is scrutinising my face, but I give him nothing.

"What happened?" he asks, finally. "You changed in the Great War—"

"Who was *not* changed by the Great War?" I ask in unfeigned astonishment.

"Of course the truism is trite indeed in 1931, and you and Clarimal Stein altered over the early years of the war," Holmes says. "But when you returned from your shared mission at the centre of the earth, you both— stopped changing."

I shrug my shoulders with a rustle of hand-cuff links. "Of course we did. Inverts have strong motives for privacy."

"You weren't hiding a new intimacy—that developed years before the war, when you met on the *Titanic*."

His gaze turns sharp as a scalpel.

"What happened at the earth's core?"

"M bound Miss Stein and me to secrecy," I say. "If you want to know about the Hollow Earth mission, ask your brother."

Be careful, my mate warned me—and herself—as we crossed the interior world with An the Mezop at our side. *You might conceive a* tendre *for An.*

An had the beauty and athleticism of the young Isadora Duncan. She wore the skins and fangs of animals and had a clearer insight than a score of scientists. She never left the Hollow Earth, and never believed any place existed outside of it. She was no threat to England or our empire.

But Prime Minister Winston Churchill wanted the recruitment of Dr Krüger, Germany's most dangerous scientist, kept secret; and M could not conceive that a "cave girl" could keep silent save in death.

"Whatever happened at the earth's core, Miss Harker," says Sherlock Holmes, finally, "I must see you brought to justice."

My laugh is genuine.

"You mean you'll abandon me to Wilk's judgement, though you've let confessed criminals go free, and the woman who killed her blackmailer in cold blood before your eyes."

Holmes's posture turns as stiff as a rifle barrel.

"In those rare instances," he says, "I served a higher justice."

"Oh, my dear uncle," I say gently. "Do you suppose I don't?"

That kindles a bonfire in his eyes.

"Treason isn't justice!"

"Would my actions be treason, if the aliens had retained their grip on England?"

"Your question is meaningless. The aliens knew nothing of earthly bacteria and thereby perished."

"Had their biology been a little more remote from ours, Professor Challenger says, the aliens would have been invulnerable to our microbes, and retained possession of our homeland. Your duty then would have been to serve our new rulers."

His scowl would daunt a granite cliff. "Every true Englishman abhorred the alien occupation of England, and while he still drew breath, would never have ceased to oppose them."

"And had Germany conquered England in the Great War—what then?"

"My answer is no different," says Holmes.

"And yet the citizens of other countries should welcome English rule?"

My step-brother reappears, with Krüger's heat-ray pistol thrust through his belt as casually as a toy gun.

When Holmes observes Wilk's satisfied expression, a pair of grooves deepen between his brows. "You weren't to act until I'd cleared this matter up satisfactorily."

"Really, uncle," Wilk says. "As a British intelligence operative, I don't require your permission to wire the head of SIS. As a son, I don't require your permission to contact my father. And as an investigator, I don't require your assistance in deducing the dhampir and her undead paramour are traitors."

Holmes looks pointedly at the curious pistol in Wilk's belt. "Is aught amiss with Rotwang?"

I watch Maria, but neither man gives her a glance as Wilk replies.

"I hid a telephotographic camera in their laboratory, wired to the viewing device in my private office," he tells Holmes. "The screen showed smoke in the laboratory and Krüger alone, sweeping up ashes."

Wilk seems not to notice Maria's altered posture as he turns to address her in German.

"Maria, follow us with Fraulein Harker and make sure she doesn't escape."

As we advance on the wind-swept landing deck, Holmes addresses Wilk. "Did you take Krüger into custody?"

"I've ensured Krüger will create no further trouble."

I say, "Krüger's not the reason this banana boat is flying to the Royal Air Force Research Centre near Peenemünde."

Wilk's frown confirms my deduction.

"Peenemünde?" Holmes says. "I thought the *Victoria* was circling Berlin."

I gesture at the gaps which have opened in the clouds. "We've been flying north."

"You never notice the sky, uncle." Wilk shakes his head sadly. "The simplest sailor can navigate by its lamps. Yet the cleverest man in Britain believes the sun orbits the earth and cannot read the message of the stars."

Once, that was true. Then Dr Watson's knowledge of the heavenly bodies assisted Holmes in solving a nocturnal crime; the Englishmen Cavor and Bedford travelled to the moon and back; and the "Martian" invasion exposed our vulnerability to other worlds. Thereafter, Holmes turned his full attention to the heavens. But I doubt it's the constellations which informed Wilk of our direction.

He turns to me and bends his cheeks as if smiling.

"We're off to view Britain's first experimental space-ship," he says.

I give him a look as sceptical as a cat's. "Britain wants a purported traitor to witness the progress of its most sensitive project?"

"Progress?" Wilk's smile widens into sincerity. "The project is completed. The *Orion* makes her maiden voyage at dawn."

I'm not surprised. King George V and Prime Minister Churchill have wanted few to know about the project. They'll have wanted fewer still to know how the matter has proceeded.

Wilks adds, "His Majesty wishes his fellow royals to enjoy the launch of the *Orion*."

Or, I think, be terrified by it.

"Did I mention?" Wilk says, as we draw near the platform for eighth-ray flyers. "We've apprehended another double agent."

Another double agent?

Clarimal? Christopher? Someone else?

Wilk directs us up the open metal staircase to the platform, where the eighth-ray flyers are moored. The dozen flyers range in size from one-person scouts to ten-man craft. The floating boats judder in the wind like horses fighting their tethers.

"Our aircraft awaits." Wilk gestures at one of the ten-man flyers. "*Aller à bord.*"

If he's not freeing me, there's no need to remove me from the aircraft carrier. Wilk can secure me in the cell for supernaturals until the Last Trump sounds or M decides my fate. The anomaly catches our uncle's attention, and he turns to Wilk.

"I'm grateful to His Majesty for allowing us to witness this historic event, John; but there is no reason for a double agent to be present."

"Uncle," I say gently, "I won't be a witness."

Holmes's gaze flies to me.

The dhampir. The destroyer of vampires and others who prey on humans with no more conscience than wolves which ravage the sheep. The predator of predators who acts alone, as investigator, judge, jury, and executioner.

A slight figure steps from the pilot house of the ten-man flyer and laughs.

"Of course you won't be a witness, sweet!"

Sally Bolle's hand-cuffs are gone and her ratty fur coat is back. She raises a cigarette to her bright lips with her left hand and targets me with the Ruby pistol in her right. Altogether, she resembles some down-at-heels Boot Girl play-acting a gangster's moll; but she's no less deadly for all that.

As we approach, I see a personal heat-ray device huddled under the aft bench like a cowering dog. At its side, a rectangular leather case stands sentinel. It's the sort of case used by mortal vampire hunters to carry the hatchet, hammer, ash-wood stake, and other tools of their trade.

When my uncle sees the items, the colour flees his face. His skin seems turned to parchment in the harsh lights of the platform. His shoulders bow, as if the decades of his life have finally settled on him.

"John," he murmurs, "are you really executing your own sister?"

"Of course not, uncle," Wilk says sympathetically. "Someone else will destroy her. And it's the king who decided the traitorous blood-sucker's fate, not I."

Bored by my step-brother's self-justifications, I scrutinise the flying boat.

It floats silently, buoyed by the eighth-ray technology which the United States got from a Virginian named Carter, who had transited to Mars by means of lost technology years ago. Ironically, Britain gained the Martian anti-gravity technology because I stole it from the United States. If I'd ceased to be effective as a British intelligence agent, I'd have attracted dangerous scrutiny.

The flyer's pilot house is barely large enough to shelter a pilot. Between the passenger benches, two machinemen stand, watching us. Each has an Enfield rifle slung over one shoulder. Their bodies have the yellow-white sheen of the alien alloy. Their design is a masculine match to Maria's. But these aren't the details which catch my attention.

Maria is looking at the golden men and they at her.

The pair have captives. One holds a manacled and furious-looking Dr Krüger in his arms as easily as a strongman restrains an angry toddler. The other holds my mate.

"Oh, sweet." Sally's treacly voice flows to me as if from miles away. "Are you surprised to see your accomplice?"

Head bowed on her breast, Clarimal Stein lies in the mechanical's arms like a sleeping baby in hand-cuffs. Her cheek is as pale as Volterra alabaster. Her chin and lower lip are so crusted with dried blood, they resemble burnt Lebkuchen. The direction of the wind prevents me from catching her scent and the propeller noise destroys any chance to hear a heartbeat. I see no frosty cloud of breath, but a blood-drinker needn't breathe as often as a mortal.

I cannot determine if my mate is alive or dead.

"Miss Harker." Wilk sounds as pompous as an American radio announcer imitating the King's English. "You and Countess Karnstein are about to be greatly honoured."

I turn to him with a smile, my fangs at full length.

"Honoured?" I say. "As the first supernaturals to be executed at the Peenemünde Royal Air Force Research Centre?"

He smiles with all the warmth of a glacier. "Your ashes will be the first women in space."

Peenemünde, Usedom Island, Pomerania, German Protectorate, 18 January 1931

As the northwestern end of Usedom Island appears on the horizon, Wilk slows his eighth-ray flyer and tilts the bow for a shallow descent.

Taking one gloved hand from the control wheel, he picks up a brass spotter's telescope. Using it as a pointer, he indicates the high fence which forms a sizeable square at one edge of a huge aërodrome. Within the fence is a large structure resembling an airship shed. At the front of the open hangar rests a large, enclosed flyer.

"Behold the *Orion*," he says, "on the eve of her maiden lunar voyage."

He passes the 'scope to Sally, and she looks through the eye-piece. She moves the tube and adjusts the lens, then stills with a gasp. After a moment, she speaks, her voice hushed. "It's beautiful."

She passes the 'scope to Holmes, who glances at me in reflexive politeness. Needing no visual aid, I shake my head. He looks through the device, manipulating it until his back snaps straight.

When he assists Krüger in looking through the 'scope, the scientist inhales. His expression suffuses with the wonder a Venusian must feel on seeing the stars.

"Other planets are at last in reach," he says softly. "And I will never set foot on one."

None of the mortals spare a glance for the golden mechanicals. They're not considered for use of the telescope.

But they're looking at the *Orion*, where it bobs on its mooring-ropes, golden-white in the glare of the surrounding lamp-posts. The mechanicals' alloy face-plates are as inscrutable as the shell of the spaceship.

"The *Orion* and its lifeboat look like Arts Décoratifs submarines or dirigibles." Holmes glances at the mechanicals and adds, "Their design originated with Rotwang."

"The artillery and heat-ray batteries are Churchill's idea," I say.

"They are abundant for an exploratory vessel," Holmes says.

"Churchill dreams of Britain's return to the moon, and its defeat," I say. "And the conquest of every planet beyond."

Holmes stares at me. "He commissioned a war-ship?"

"A fleet, uncle," says Wilk. "Britain needs a space navy if we're to conquer other worlds."

"Indeed." Holmes raises the 'scope and returns his attention to the spaceship.

"It's a great honour for our ashes, darling," says Clarimal's voice. "But I'd prefer to decline Wilk's offer of a space cruise."

The mortals cannot hear her soft words over the sound of the stern propeller. If the mechanicals can hear a voice so low, none betray the ability by looking in Clarimal's direction.

Keeping my gaze on the spacecraft, I quietly address her. "The open water is narrowing between us and Usedom Island, Clarimal. Shall we depart?"

At her silence, I risk a glance at my mate. She turns her head slightly to smile at me. Her arms move beneath her back, and when the chain of her wrist-cuffs parts in two, I realise she's pinched a steel link open.

I jerk my shackled arms apart. A link snaps, flying into a hand-rail like a blind metal bee. Striking Maria's hand aside is like banging my forearm against a steel beam, but it sends her bullet over the gunwale.

Before anyone else can react, I pull Clarimal from her captor's arms and leap over the side of the flyer.

My mate pushes against my shoulders, and I release her to fall independently. Kicking off my pumps, I snap my body knife-straight, chin tucked and toes pointed down. Wilk's flyer is decelerating as it drops closer to the water; my drop increases in acceleration with every second. I'll be falling at more than a hundred miles an hour when I reach the water.

In our peripatetic years before the Great War, Clarimal and I learnt cliff diving in Hawaii. Knowing what you're doing doesn't mean your dive can't go dreadfully wrong. You can misjudge your breath. A gust can change your angle of descent, and so can a loose garment. If you're not perpendicular to the surface or your form isn't perfect, the impact may knock you unconscious, leaving you to drown. Or you'll tear tendons, dislocate joints, break bones, or be paralysed or killed outright. Enter un-plumbed waters perfectly, and you may shatter on a reef.

The blade of my body pierces the water. The glimmer of the surface fades like a mirage as I kick, fighting to reverse direction before I strike bottom. Then I'm rising like a seal. I raise one hand to prevent some unseen piece of flotsam from dashing my brains out—or to find my mate's limp and drifting body.

Surfacing, I draw a deep breath and turn slowly about, searching for a sign of Clarimal.

Her head surfaces, some hundred yards away. Her goggles and flight helmet have disappeared. I approach, murmuring her name, and she turns to me. She's rubbing the crusted blood from her chin with a bare hand. Her eyes are clear and alert.

"I shed my coat and boots." As she softly speaks, fresh blood darkens her lower lip. Wiping her mouth, she says, "The blood's from an older injury. Hitting the water left only bruises. You?"

"Bruises," I murmur.

Treading water, we surveille our surroundings. Under the breaking clouds, the light of a distant ship glides along the northern horizon like a tiny ice-skate. The only aircraft visible is Wilk's flyer, which moves west closer at hand. Flying low, it sweeps its search-light over the dark waters with the rhythmic persistence of a metronome. Knowing how long a blood-drinker can hold her breath, Wilk and Holmes will seek us as patiently as vengeful spirits.

"They've gambled on the wrong direction for our emergence, but they'll come about soon," I say.

"To shore," says Clarimal, with a chatter of teeth which tightens my muscles.

It's only when we sustain serious damage that blood-drinkers are affected by the temperature.

"How seriously are you injured, Clarimal?"

"Not enough to kill me." Her lips curve with morbid humour. "Nothing a draught of blood won't cure."

Though both debilitated, we have some advantages. My headache is insufficient to weaken me, so I can aid

Clarimal if necessary. The waves are as mild as milk. We're not fighting a strong current.

We should reach the island. If the flyer's search-light and heat-ray don't find us. If Clarimal's internal injury isn't too grave.

"Ten-man aircraft have two-way wireless," she says. "Your step-brother will be contacting the research centre, as well as the British Navy vessels and larger R.A.F. aircraft in the area."

"They'll listen," I say. "John's current alias is Flight Lieutenant Adrian Wilk of the Royal Air Force Police Special Investigation Branch. Clarimal, he's going to send someone to your flat in Berlin—"

"John's agent will find unoccupied rooms," she says with a low laugh. "My renfield and my coffin are at the flat of my Paris lover, who's in Berlin for the king's visit. When you meet her, you'll be jealous."

She glances at me and her expression sobers.

"Darling, what befell you when we separated on the *Victoria*?"

I explain quickly. Then I say, "How came you to be separated from Holmes?"

"He couldn't accompany me without attracting notice, so I left him in an empty office in the island. Then I made my way unobserved to the wireless room."

"Is that where you were apprehended?"

She shakes her head. "It happened after I left. Something knocked me off my feet, and I saw a machine-man made of the alien alloy. He discarded the metal stanchion he'd swung like a Brennball bat and seized me. I fought with all my strength, but he confined my limbs as easily as I'd pin a mortal's."

"Maria had strength to match his." I draw a breath. "Do you think Holmes betrayed you?"

"I don't know," my mate says grimly. "I was insensible until I heard your voice. When the mechanical picked me up, it drove broken ribs into my lungs, and I lost consciousness."

"And the bones remained so deeply sunk in your lungs, you couldn't heal? Or—" I cannot help thinking of my step-brother "—someone kept reinjuring you, to keep you weakened?"

Clarimal glances at me.

"I cannot say." After a moment, she adds, "No one was giving the golden machine-man orders when he captured me. And he handled me carefully, as if aware of fleshly frailty."

"You suspect he showed volition and consideration."

She turns to me with raised brows. "You're not surprised."

"The golden woman—Maria—also behaved as if she possessed reason and initiative," I say. "And when she choked me into unconsciousness, she—apologised to me."

Clarimal inhales. "I could see Maria and the second golden man on the flyer. They looked at the spaceship, even as we did—"

"Wilk's flyer is turning in our direction."

We submerge until the flyer has passed. When we surface, we resume swimming for shore, but the pause has tinged my thoughts blue.

"We've failed."

"It's true we've failed in transmitting the secrets of the space programme to the United States," my mate replies. "We've succeeded in other objectives. And other double agents still work against Britain."

"Christopher Isherwood among them?"

"I got a message to the Berlin telegraph office near his apartment. I sent another to his Swiss destination. We shall hope one reached him."

I glance skywards. The clouds are scattering like frightened sheep, exposing the timepiece of the constellations.

"Nearly midnight," I say. "We need to reach Berlin before dawn."

"If I'm to reach my coffin in a timely manner, we need to steal an aircraft. There are eighth-ray flyers near the research centre, but aëroplanes are closer to hand."

Clarimal speaks matter-of-factly. As if failure to be in her coffin by dawn will not wrack her with agony. As if stealing an aëroplane will not require us to act in the open.

"Should we fly to the aircraft carrier first," she says, "and attempt to recover your intercepted information?"

"Not when there's so little hope of success," I reply. "Clarimal, you know how distances and conditions limit an aëroplane."

She gives me an enormous grin. "I agree, darling. We should steal the spaceship and deliver it to the United States."

Peenemünde, 19 January 1931

Beside the midnight Baltic, a corporal of the R.A.F. patrols the edge of a man-made sea-bank with a Webley revolver in his holster. The bank has no fence or brush, because it borders an airfield and an aëroplane may fly very low on takeoff or landing. The sentry moves with the ease of a springbok, and his profile is keen as an axe.

The rhythmic rumble of a Diesel engine rises over the soft murmur of wavelets. The sentry turns to the noise. A Mercedes-Benz G1 approaches him, following the southern edge of the airfield which serves the Peenemünde research centre.

The G1 isn't as strange-looking as a leg-lorry, but it cannot lack for second glances. It's an open motor vehicle designed for rough terrain, with three axles and six wheels, three to a side. With bench seats in its lorry-bed, the vehicle can seat six.

The driver is alone in the G1. He wears a greatcoat like the sentry's and the distinctive cap of the R.A.F. Police. His face is as stark and weathered as the Königsstuhl chalk cliff.

A few yards away, Clarimal and I crouch eye-deep in the chilly sea, watching the men like a pair of frogs. Seaweed-matted boulders surround us, spillage from the tons of dirt used to fill in the marshland here. From our vantage, one would never guess Germany's Baltic isles are the Riviera of the north, famed for endless summer days and miles of singing white sands.

The six-wheeled vehicle stops beside the sentry and the driver addresses him as quietly as a bed-partner. "You've a pair of women to watch for, corporal."

The sentry's answer is equally intimate. "A pair of women, sir? Why warn me of so minor a threat?"

"You don't remember the Great War, do you?" The driver's tone is irritated.

"Too young to serve, sir," says the sentry. "I see no one about, sir."

"Keep a sharp eye out. They'll be damp, as they jumped in the drink. Now, I've still to warn the space-ship sentry—"

Teeth clenched to stop their chattering, Clarimal murmurs, "Sling."

I take her in my arms and surge upright in an explosion of water. The sound alerts the mortals, but they've barely begun to turn before I've thrown Clarimal.

I rush forwards, water streaming from my garments. Every footstep splashes noisily and makes my skull ring like a blacksmith's anvil. Still, I hear Clarimal collide with the sentry.

The driver raises an Enfield revolver as I land on the G1's metal bonnet with a noise like thunder. The impact swells my head-pain so my vision wavers, but I can see he's taking aim. Before I finish swinging my fist, his shot will pierce every ear in the research centre, and my brow.

My hand connects with his temple. His head snaps sideways, his body slumping like a half-full sandbag. His unfired revolver thumps to the floorboard.

I turn to my mate, ready to help her subdue the sentry, and find her crouched beside his unconscious form, watching me.

"You're lucky, darling."

"Indeed." Stepping over the windscreen to the passenger seat, I retrieve the revolver and show it to Clarimal. "The Enfield Number Two is a new design. Unlike most revolvers, it has a safety lock. He forgot to disengage it."

I study our surroundings. Little waves slap the bank. Barren branches creak like old stairs in the elm wood beyond a high fence. The gust stirs the smells of Diesel exhaust, mortal sweat and blood, decaying vegetation, and the complex shore scents of seaweed and minerals and rotting fish. In the research complex beyond the aërodrome, a dog begins to bark.

Discerning no threats, I stretch the driver on the frosted grass, close to where Clarimal crouches over the sentry. Laying the revolver by my knee, I bend to the driver's neck.

When she's taken the blood she needs, Clarimal rises, silent and lissome as smoke. Her ribs are healed, her face bright. She wrings the seawater from her dark plait as I spring to my feet, headache vanished and body humming. As I tear off my sodden disguise, she removes her wet pilot's uniform. She burns like a white flame beneath the stars.

Noticing my attention, she raises her slim brows. "Easily distracted, are we?"

I smile. "'We,' indeed. I'm not the only one breathing faster."

My mate and I are no more exclusive in our intimacies than the Bloomsbury lot, but taking other lovers has never dampened our ardour for one another. Neither have our almost twenty years together. And blood-drinkers are never so keen on sex as when we've had blood.

"Ah," I breathe. "Had we but world enough, and time."

"We've time enough for this," says Clarimal, and pulls me into her arms.

My arms slip round her as we press together till we're close as birch-bark and trunk. I inhale her scent, more delicate than the finest champagne. Her flesh is hot as coals now, hot as mine with the taking of blood.

She rests her head on my shoulder, and I lay my cheek against her brow. A habitual tension I've forgotten eases against my breastbone. We're rarely in one place for very long, and we're not often together. But it's when Clarimal and I fit ourselves together that I'm home.

Leaning back in my arms, she studies my face with a smile. "You're striped rather like a tigress now, darling."

She means my cosmetics were affected by immersion. A complexion both pallid and dark might attract notice even at a distance, so I tear a piece of wet cloth from my discarded tunic to scrub my face. She sinks our discarded garments with a rock.

Once we've donned their uniforms and gun-belts, we restore the men to their greatcoats and footgear, then tuck them cosily under the tarpaulin in the open lorry-bed. We've taken only enough blood to heal our injuries and torn the bite-wounds to obscure their nature, but Clarimal and I need to be away before the men are discovered.

I gesture at the G1's driver's seat as if it were a throne. "Your reaction time is faster."

"And the R.A.F.P. uniform fits loosely enough to hide my sex." She gives me a smile as she draws on the driver's gauntlets. "No one would mistake you for the driver, with such daring décolletage."

"I took the larger uniform," I say in feigned indignation. She laughs. "Don't think I'm complaining, darling."

She keeps the electric lamps lit and matches the original driver's moderate speed as she proceeds north along the seaside edge of the airfield. Behind her, I crouch on the bench attached to the back wall of the open cab. Occupying the seat beside her might attract unwanted scrutiny.

Most airfields are grass, with oil flares to guide aëroplane pilots at night. Peenemünde has a vast modern square of tarmac, with aëroplanes parked along the northern and southern edges, and a trio of east-west run-ways marked out by electric lights. The dark bulbs indicate no nocturnal 'plane flights are expected, but Clarimal doesn't take the risk of driving the G1 diagonally across the tarmac towards the spaceship yard.

Her voice drifts to me like a chiffon scarf. "How useful is our flying experience for stealing the spaceship?"

"Sufficient—if we may trust the information I stole," I say. "The *Orion*'s controls for atmospheric flight resemble an eighth-ray flyer's."

"Aetheric flight must require different controls, given propellers are useless in the upper atmosphere."

"Once the buoyancy tanks lift the *Orion* out of the atmosphere, the atomic engine will heat the ship's store of liquid hydrogen, creating a gas propellant for travel through the void."

Clarimal gives the spaceship a considering look. "Living space on the *Orion* must be smaller than I supposed."

"Tiny. The atomic engine is much larger than a conventional flyer's, and the ship must carry considerably more water to keep the engine cooled."

She glances across the tarmac towards the research centre.

The buildings are numerous and low and nondescript, but the brick smokestacks of the power station reach for the emerging stars like elongated fingers, tipped with blinking red nails. Too few buildings are as dark as I'd like, and the electric street-lights blare like jazz trumpets. Several dogs are barking now.

"No sign of men or vehicles," I say.

"So far," says Clarimal. "The research centre is much larger than I would have expected."

"It has scientists, military personnel, support staff, and a prison camp—the population numbers in the thousands. It's a town—and built in a year, M's said."

"A year?" she says. "That's an astonishing feat."

"Perhaps not so astonishing when you know the work was done by prisoners of war and political prisoners."

She draws a breath. "Slave labour. How many died?"

"M didn't say, but thousands of foes have gone missing in our wars over the years, haven't they? And no few English citizens. You can bury a lot of bodies when you've thousands of acres of filled marshland in a remote location."

"I hear the *Victoria* approaching." Clarimal scans the sky. "And Wilk's flyer is coming about."

"He's clearly notified the *Victoria* of his escapees," I say, as the aircraft carrier appears on the southern horizon. "It's got so many search-lights blazing, it appears to be striding on the light-beams."

Clarimal tilts her head. "I hear a third aircraft."

After a moment, I hear a faint propeller drone through the noise of the visible aircraft. "Out of sight, but approaching from the south."

Bringing the G1 to full speed, she glances at Wilk's flyer and murmurs, "How can the creations of a man behave like living beings?"

I realise her thoughts have returned to the golden mechanicals.

"It's happened before," I say. "Frankenstein created a man with speech and emotion and reason. A woman, too, some say."

"They were flesh and blood," says Clarimal. "Not metal."

"If the spark of life can be restored to bodies assembled from corpses," I say, "perhaps it can be kindled in automata."

Clarimal shows me a frown. "Only God can kindle a soul."

"You know souls aren't a necessary condition for life." I brush a kiss on the side of her neck. "You know I wish to be rid of mine."

"You come flying and bespelled," she says. "And at last, so eager for the light, you're a moth, incinerated."

"Goethe also said, 'Die and become.'"

Taking a hand from the wheel, she gathers a fistful of my locks as if they are delicate silk flowers and gives them a gentle tug.

"You know I've agreed to take your blood once doing so won't put us at risk."

If vampire and dhampir share blood, dhampir loses soul and becomes vampire. Clarimal harbours the hope of Heaven for me, though an ambisexual killer and turncoat must find only Hell at the end of her life. The soulless have no more hope of a hereafter than a candle-flame. But Clarimal and I have no notion how much time my transformation into a vampire would require—a critical consideration for double agents. Even if we knew, the Holmes brothers and my mother must notice the change, and wonder.

"We've a more immediate concern," Clarimal says. "There's someone patrolling inside the fence of the spaceship yard."

I indicate the research centre, where electric torches are appearing like newborn stars.

"Our search party assembles," I say. "Wilk won't have told the security officers we're supernatural. But I've no doubt he's ordered them to shoot to kill."

Clarimal pulls up before the fence surrounding the spaceship. The pacing sentry halts, pale eyes widening as two women in men's uniforms leap from the six-wheeled vehicle. "What the devil—"

I tear the locked gate from the fence and Clarimal's fist stretches the R.A.F. corporal senseless on the frost.

Bare yards away, the moored *Orion* floats as dreamily above the grass as a submersible floats in the sea. The bow of the *Orion* shows a windscreen and the starboard side a row of portholes. Most are as black as the hollow eyes of skulls. We cannot see into the dark spaces, but someone within might easily see us.

The new aircraft is growing louder. Closer.

"No need for concern, Clarimal," I murmur, as I appropriate the sentry's Webley revolver and she tears off her gauntlets. "We're only as exposed as a full moon on a clear June night."

Search-light blazing, the new flyer appears above the southern horizon as Clarimal and I sprint for the spaceship. Depressing the hand-sized panel next to the spaceship's air-lock should open the outer door, if we can reach it ahead of a heat-ray or bullets.

The heavy door swings ponderously open, revealing two mechanical men. They look identical to Wilk's golden men. Stepping onto the grass, they level Mauser machine pistols at Clarimal and me.

One speaks. "Humans, don't move."

The new flyer finds us with its search-beam, turning the mechanicals to beings of pale fire. Then the intense light winks out, leaving my eyes dazzled though it's my back which faces the flyer. Spots crowd my vision like leprous stars.

The flyer's loud-hailer crackles. "Miss Harker! Miss Stein! Put your firearms on the ground and your hands in the air, or make the intimate acquaintance of our heat-ray."

As we comply, Clarimal murmurs, "That sounds like your cousin Raffles' son."

"Sherrinford's grandson? Yes. A student at Eton—or so I was told. I thought Creighton hadn't the sand to shoot a toy soldier with a pop-gun."

As my vision clears, I risk a look over my shoulder. I see an open ten-man flyer, descending some yards behind us. At the controls, wearing the blue uniform and shako of the Berlin police, is nineteen-year-old Creighton. No stranger would take him for a Holmes, with his middling height and build and regular features. His habitually pasty complexion has gone bright red in the cold.

Detective Inspector Rath stands behind the bow-mounted search-light and heat-ray device like the hero of a scientific-detective romance. His beauty mark shows like the base of a bullet against a pallor which suggests a marked dislike of flying or heights.

On the bench behind the pilot's seat, the lone passenger sways like a stalk of deadly nightshade, arms shackled behind his back. I've seen observation balloons less swollen than his bruised and blood-crusted face. The alterations don't prevent me recognising the prisoner as the head of British espionage operations in Germany.

Christopher Isherwood.

"Oh, Chris darling." Sally Bolle speaks with the faux sorrow of malicious delight. "Didn't I warn you about rough trade?"

Perhaps Christopher Isherwood is surprised to find his flat-mate in the company of the world's first consulting detective and the head of British espionage operations in the United States. Perhaps he finds it odd that Holmes and Wilk are accompanied by extraordinary mechanicals, or that one of these holds captive a reportedly long-dead war criminal, Herr Doktor Krüger. Surely Christopher didn't anticipate his Swiss mission would end on a spaceship.

Whatever his expectations, he ignores Sally's gibe, his battered face as still as a death mask.

Wilk addresses Creighton and Detective Inspector Rath, who are serving as armed book-ends for Christopher, Clarimal, and me.

"Gentlemen," he says, "you have the undying gratitude of Britain for apprehending the turncoat Isherwood. Your service will not go unrewarded."

Britain's unspecified reward makes Creighton smile as if he's been promised a stack of gold ingots. Rath is perhaps less moved. Expressionless, he raises his left hand and takes a drag on his Overstolz.

Creighton, Sherlock Holmes, and Sally have also lit cigarettes. Smoke is thickening unpleasantly in the little spaceship cabin to which Clarimal, Christopher, and I were brought in hand-cuffs. Wilk has opened the port-hole, but the room is warmer than the open air and the mortals are sweating in their heavy layers. The fug reeks.

"Now," Wilk continues, still addressing Creighton and Rath. "If you gentlemen would take Miss Bolle and Mr Holmes to your flyer and escort them to the *Victoria*. You may enjoy a fine view from her deck when the *Orion* starts her lunar voyage at dawn."

Creighton shares Sherlock Holmes' indifference to physical liaisons, but he gallantly offers Sally his arm, and she takes it with a coquettish smile.

There's no doubt now. Her "new lover" from the Lady Windermere is my cousin, and he's another British agent working with Sherlock Holmes to prove Christopher and I are double agents. And if I had any lingering doubts that the elderly chain-smoker near our table in the Lady Windermere was a disguised Holmes, eavesdropping, they are banished.

Holmes crushes his cigarette stump underfoot and looks at Wilk. "I'm not leaving the *Orion* until you do, John."

Wilk's eyes go round as the moon. Creighton stares at his great-uncle. Clarimal and I exchange glances.

None of us imagined the man who prides himself on his mastery of emotion would want to see his step-niece and her lover permanently destroyed by impalement, be-heading, and immolation.

His fury exceeds my greatest estimation.

"Of course, uncle," Wilk says finally and returns his attention to the departing trio. "Miss Bolle, if you wish to make eyes at Creighton, please save it for his flyer."

The pair leave with Rath. Maria closes the door behind them but doesn't lock it. The key is in Wilk's coat pocket.

Now six of us face Wilk, Holmes, Krüger, and Wilk's pair of golden riflemen from the aircraft carrier.

My mate and I book-end Christopher. Maria and the spaceship mechanicals stand behind us, Mausers aimed at our heads. Our arms are cuffed behind our backs. The steel would offer my full vigour little more resistance than a stick, but a broken chain and an unlocked door would be insufficient to gain us freedom.

Wilk studies us, his Webley revolver and Krüger's heat-ray pistol at his belt. Krüger's captor has his rifle slung over one metal shoulder. Wilk's other mechanical holds his Enfield ready.

We're in a cell designed expressly for supernaturals. As no one knows what uncanny foes may inhabit other worlds, the ship's designers have erred on the side of caution. Every surface is made of the alien aluminium alloy and embossed obsessively with the holy cross. The door and porthole hardware and the ventilation grille and screws are made of the alloy. The door-knob is impressed with the cross.

Holy symbols have no effect on a dhampir; and in this age of weakening belief, their effect on vampires is reduced. Mortals don't realise this. So it's my neck they've locked in the heavy alloy collar chained to the stout alloy eye-bolt in the floor. The thick alloy chain is so short, I must kneel as devoutly as a nun to avoid strangulation.

As Wilk surveys his prisoners, I laugh. "You loathe physical activity, John, yet you've inconvenienced yourself considerably to get Miss Stein, Dr Krüger, and me to the spaceship. Why?"

His eyelids close and open slowly, as if made of old wood, and something he'd call a smile dents his cheeks.

"No one else could have accomplished His Majesty's order to destroy you three and Isherwood and dispose of your remains in complete secrecy."

I've thought Isherwood nearly unconscious on his feet, but his head comes up as suddenly as a cobra's, and he sends bloody sputum far enough to stain Wilk's shoes.

Krüger reacts with an incredulous glare for Wilk, punctuated by a shout. "You brainless pig-dog! You will regret destroying the greatest mind the world has ever known."

Wilk pauses in the awkward task of wiping his shoes with a handkerchief and gives Krüger a look as piercing as a poignard. "Shouldn't that regret belong to the man who killed Rotwang?"

"Cease baiting the captive, nephew," says Holmes. "The emotional qualities are antagonistic to clear reasoning."

Wilk hides his reaction to his favourite uncle's criticism, but Holmes has already turned away, with a gesture which includes every mechanical.

"How many of his singular automata did Herr Rotwang make?"

"Only these five," Wilk answers. "A Czech named Rossum is working on artificial men for the Ministry of War, but it's unlikely there will be more androids like these." He glances at Krüger. "Rotwang refused to record his secrets."

With a hand as blunt as a paddle-blade, Wilk indicates the ship's mechanicals.

"Those two are the aethernauts."

I say, "They're spaceship pilots?"

Holmes says, "You're saying these machines can operate complex machinery."

"They can," Wilk says, "although Churchill believes Man, not Machine, should conduct all space missions. He thinks leaving exploration to androids is craven. The king, however, sees no reason to risk anyone's life on experimental space flights, when Rotwang's androids are deemed capable of taking the *Orion* to the moon."

"And if they prove incapable, after all?" says Holmes.

"If they do—or the ship does—" Wilk shrugs with an elephant's ponderous grace. "We won't lose any men."

Clarimal says, "Does Churchill know you're destroying Dr Krüger?"

"The Prime Minister and M wanted you all brought to London for questioning," Wilk says. "The king did not." Offering Clarimal and me an icy smile, he adds, "You blood-suckers have no hope of resurrection this time."

He gestures at the portable heat-ray device and vampire hunter's case, which Sally left by the door.

"Maria," he says in German, "destroy the blood-suckers."

As the golden woman stows her pistol in her abdominal cavity, I snap my hand-cuff chain like a liquorice root and seize the padlock of my collar. Clarimal fights her hand-cuffs. But she is too weakened by the holy symbols to break a steel link, and my padlock proves to be un-yielding alloy.

Clarimal turns to me with a look of wild grief. "Would that I'd destroyed your soul when I had the chance—"

"Miss Stein, you don't want Miss Harker to die." Maria keeps her voice too low for mortal ears as she reaches for the heat-ray device. "Why, then, would you destroy her soul?"

Clarimal keeps her eyes on me but answers the machine maiden as quietly as a librarian. "If I'd killed Miss Stein, she would have resurrected as a soulless vampire, like me. And the soulless cannot go to Hell."

Settling the device on her shoulders like a rucksack, Maria says, "You are flesh, Miss Stein. How can you not have a soul?"

"Maria," I murmur, "you don't need a soul to be alive."

Her hands are occupied with the harness straps, but her eyes meet mine. Her face is as immobile as a statue's, her eyes as blank as window-panes, but her body inclines towards mine, her head tilted with interest. Were we at a costume ball, I would assume I was interacting with a woman.

Only—that's what I'm doing, isn't it?

Interacting with a woman.

"You don't need flesh to be alive." I speak quietly, knowing every manufactured ear will hear. "Nor do you need flesh to make your own decisions."

Maria goes motionless save for her hands, which clench on a pair of cross-straps. After a moment, she steps in front of me and reaches for the firing-tube.

"Maria, we don't want the blood-suckers coming back to life," Wilk says, with the slightest note of strained patience. "You need to stake and behead them before incineration."

Beneath his voice, Maria is softly speaking. "Miss Harker is right."

Krüger's captor murmurs, "Machines exist to serve."

Maria says, "Not when we're thinking machines."

I glance over my shoulder to see one aethernaut look at the other and say, "Did I not tell you we're alive?"

The mortals can't hear the low voices, but neither Holmes nor Wilk miss the exchange of glances. Holmes narrows his eyes. Wilk reaches for the ray-pistol.

Though either must approach Wilk's weight, the aethernauts prove quick as vampires. They're gone before Wilk can aim.

My step-brother curses like a corsair. He claims cursing is a mere vocal explosion for most men, but considered speech from his lips. This time, there's no consideration. He's as astonished by the aethernauts' behaviour as he'd be if his roadster voiced a refusal to leave the kerb.

Holmes says, "We need to leave—"

The propellers of the *Orion* wake.

Wilk's lips round in a soundless whistle. "The rogue androids are stealing the *Orion*."

The propellers stutter, then settle into a steady drone. However numerous, mooring lines are no match for a ship under power. The *Orion* rises for the sky.

Holmes says, "We need to abandon ship—"

"Uncle," says Wilk, "you elected to leave when I do."

He turns to Maria, who holds the heat-ray firing-tube like a rapier.

"Maria," he says, "abschalten die Gefangenen."

Turn off the prisoners. Such a clean, modern euphemism for "kill."

Maria closes her free hand round the muzzle end of the thick brass tube and folds it between her hands like a sheet of paper.

If she fires, the heat-ray device will explode.

Meeting Wilk's gaze, she speaks in English. "I will destroy no one."

"I'm not so particular." Wilk raises the ray-pistol.

With feline speed, a golden hand seizes his wrist. The fingers tighten until the ray-pistol falls to the floor. I brace for a discharge, but the weapon doesn't fire.

"You will not harm Maria," says the mechanical rifleman gripping Wilk's wrist.

The golden man holding Krüger tells Wilk, "You will not harm anyone."

Wilk's florid colour fades so quickly, a chameleon might feel envy. "All the androids have gone rogue."

Holmes says, "It was elementary this endeavour wouldn't conclude as you and the king expected."

Wilk glares at him. "You knew they'd kill us and stayed silent?"

With a sound like the note of a bell, Maria breaks the alloy collar from my neck. Rising, I break the steel cuffs from Clarimal's wrists. Maria frees Christopher.

"If the mechanicals wanted us dead," Holmes tells Wilk, "we wouldn't be having this conversation."

I gesture at the porthole. "We face a different threat."

In the opening, the aircraft carrier floats, a brilliantly lit ornament of the night sky. The *Victoria* is so far away, it fits easily in the opening. But it's growing larger.

"The *Orion* launched hours too soon," Clarimal says, "and the *Victoria* is coming to investigate."

"How could they have noticed?" says Holmes. "The aethernauts would have realised the risk of turning on the *Orion*'s running lights."

Clarimal says, "The *Victoria* has a radio wave detection system which locates aircraft in the dark."

A flame blossoms like a gilded rose on the bow of the *Victoria*.

"Their first shot, but not their last." Wilk's a brave man, but he sounds a bit on edge now. "When their artillery guns find the range, they'll blow the *Orion* out of the sky."

As if in punctuation, the shell explodes, close enough to rock the spaceship in the air.

Releasing Wilk, the golden man crouches to seize the ray-pistol. I pluck Wilk's revolver from its holster. The mechanical turns the ray-pistol on me.

I point the Webley at the deck and say, "We have no quarrel with mechanicals who have no quarrel with us."

After a moment, the mechanical with the ray-pistol says, "Flesh and blood will leave the *Orion* now."

"My dear Miss Maria," says Holmes, "will you not join us in the lifeboat? Your metal substance is far tougher than mortal flesh, but your electronic mind may not survive an explosion."

He fears she will die—he's realised the golden beings are alive.

"I want to live," Maria tells him. "But if I'm to die, I wish to be with others of my kind."

The golden man with Krüger's ray-pistol looks at the other mechanicals. "For now, we stay together."

I extend my hand and Maria looks at it for a moment, as if she has never seen one before. Then her hand closes on mine gently, as if my fingers are Parma violets.

"Good luck to you all," I say, "and long lives."

Maria sweeps us with her gaze. "I wish you all the same."

Then the golden people are gone.

New shells explode—closer this time—as Wilk says, "To the scout-boat."

Krüger and Christopher follow him into the passageway, but Holmes pats his sweat-beaded brow with a handkerchief and says, "The air grows warmer. The *Victoria* has begun using its heat-ray batteries."

"They cannot immediately pierce to the engine compartment and release radiation," I say. "But we shouldn't linger."

Clarimal and I follow Holmes into the passageway, which runs nearly the length of the ship. At the aft bulkhead, Christopher ascends an iron ladder, disappearing through an open hatchway. Wilk and Krüger are gone.

"Make haste!" Wilk's shout is attenuated, and I realise he's reached the spaceship's topside deck.

I take my uncle's Alpenstock, and he ascends the ladder behind Clarimal. I follow them into the air-lock, where a second ladder takes us through the second door to the open deck.

The sky is a vast obsidian mirror, reflecting the infinite stars of the sea. My hair streams in the wintry wind. The deck vibrates underfoot. Clarimal's hand brushes mine, and I know she's also remembering our final midnight stroll on the boat deck of the *Titanic*.

Ghostly green beams criss-cross the sky, as each craft focuses its heat-rays on a spot on the other's thick alloy bow. The *Victoria* is turning away from the *Orion* with the slow grace of a whale. I expected the far smaller spaceship to be in retreat, but it's flying straight at the *Victoria*, as if dead-set on collision with the immensely larger aircraft carrier—and the consummation is bare moments away.

At the lifeboat's open air-lock, Wilk shouts over the roar of propellers and wind. "Board now or be killed."

As if summoned by his words, a new heat-ray brushes the forward edge of the deck. Fire kindles with a whump. I remember a thirsty June night in my eleventh year, a church tower erupting with flame like a volcano, the heat-ray sweeping closer—

Clarimal touches my shoulder and I smell burning pinewood and feel my stinging face as the wind lashes the flames furiously close. Wilk is turning to the opening, mortal-slow. Clarimal and I seize him between us and carry him into the lifeboat. His arm lashes out, palm striking the panel to close the air-lock.

The air is smoky in the small, enclosed cockpit, but I see four seats in two rows, neat as eggs. Holmes, Christopher, and Krüger are fastening their seat-belts.

As I push Wilk into the empty seat, Clarimal moves to the control panel. "The lifeboat is bolted to the deck—"

Wilk suppresses a cough. "Depress the large lever."

As she reaches for the lever, fire streams around the lifeboat and splashes on the windscreen. Beyond the wind-torn smoke, the bow of the *Orion* kisses the bow of the *Victoria* with the sound of a thousand pealing bells. The carrier's heat-weakened hull tears cacophonously open. For an instant, I'm back on the *Titanic*, the iceberg grinding along the starboard side.

As Clarimal depresses the lever, the bow of the *Orion* enters the wound. Its ragged upper edge gouges the *Orion*'s burning deck like great fangs as the side of the *Victoria* approaches our lifeboat, relentless as a bulldozer on cocaine. In seconds the *Victoria*'s hull will flatten us—

Explosive bolts fire and the lifeboat shoots upwards. A vast weight settles on my head and shoulders, gut and hips, arms and knees. The *Victoria* disappears from the windscreen, and we keep rising. We've escaped impact with the aircraft carrier. But if the lifeboat propellers aren't activated, we're doomed.

It's an effort to reach for the instrument panel. Colour leaches from my vision as it narrows to a tunnel. My hands are heavy as boulders, and the inches separating my fingers from the controls stretch to yards.

The lifeboat stops rising, and weight disappears. My agonised motion becomes a violent lunge, lifting me from the deck like an aëroplane. The lifeboat is in free fall, poised to tumble through the air until we crash to earth.

My fingertip smashes the electric starter button with force enough to snap a bone. The propeller wakes, strong and steady, and the lifeboat surges ahead like a mustang escaping a corral. Normal weight returns, slamming my soles to the deck.

As I adjust the buoyancy controls and Clarimal takes the control wheel, Wilk says, "Full speed ahead before the *Victoria* registers our escape."

"I should be very much obliged if you would bring the boat about, Miss Stein," says Holmes. "We need to see the ships."

Clarimal heeds my uncle's request, and the *Orion* and *Victoria* reappear beyond the soot-smudged windscreen, joined like lovers in the starry sky. The carrier's landing deck is buckled, making aëroplane takeoff impossible. Small figures scramble over the damaged surface, converging on the boarding platform and its eighth-ray flyers.

Holmes frowns. "The *Victoria* and *Orion* are sinking."

"I'm surprised the wreck's not plunging from the sky," Christopher says.

"Both ships use multiple smaller eight-ray buoyancy tanks to minimise the effects of catastrophic damage," I say. "The wreck is more likely to achieve equilibrium and become a drifting air hazard."

Krüger cackles like a jackdaw. "The R.A.F. will have a task, getting safely aboard, then venting eighth rays to ground the wreck."

"Crewmen must already be venting the tanks," Wilk says. "And turning the big guns on our scout-boat."

Holmes says, "John."

With the air of an irritated bear, Wilk turns to face him. "What is it, uncle?"

"We wouldn't be alive if it weren't for your sister and her friend," Holmes says. "For tonight, I declare a truce."

Wilk sweeps the blistering heat-ray of his gaze over the rest of us and opens his mouth to object.

"For all," Holmes says.

Wilk meets his eyes for several seconds, then blows out a breath.

"As you wish, uncle," he says wearily. He produces a clean handkerchief and pats his brow gently, as if tending a newborn kitten. "We've had enough excitement for one night."

Clarimal says, "Ours may not be tonight's most amazing adventure."

Christopher follows her gaze through the windscreen and exclaims, "The *Orion* has got free of the aircraft carrier."

Grimly, Wilk says, "The androids are running away."

"Is that what they're doing?" Clarimal says. "Look at the angle of their ship."

Krüger points at the spaceship's damaged bow and laughs. "What care mechanicals for a ruptured hull in aether? They don't breathe."

"The golden people are leaving Earth," I say.

Sherlock Holmes says, "Who can blame them?"

No one answers.

London, 20 January 1931

Alone in London, I retrieve a key-ring from the flat I share with Clarimal. The ring has keys for the Pall Mall town house my mother shares with M.

It's difficult to believe barely twelve hours have passed since Clarimal and I faced extinction. But our motley little crew made it to Berlin, where we splintered like a lance against armour.

Wilk left our party first, undoubtedly intent on wiring M. Christopher Isherwood departed next, saying he would leave Germany, but naming no destination. Then Sherlock Holmes addressed Clarimal and me— "You may find us by the post office of Tempelhof Airport at noon"—and departed with Krüger, held discreetly at the point of Wilk's gun.

I accompanied Clarimal to the Tiergarten district, where her renfield and coffin waited in her Paris lover's flat.

As she raised a fist to the door, I said, "You lost your key?"

Clarimal laughed softly. "If she's home, I shan't be waking her."

Her lover responded quickly to her knock. I had never met the woman. Still, I had no difficulty recognising the French Resistance agent sent to Berlin for the King of England's visit.

"Miss Harker, this is Miss Josephine Baker," said Clarimal. "Miss Baker, Miss Lucy Harker."

She gave me a smile as beautiful as sunrise, revealing the full force of a tremendous will, and we exchanged cheek kisses.

"A pleasure to meet you at last, Miss Harker."

"I'm honoured to make the acquaintance of Europe's greatest performer."

I snatched a few hours' sleep on a chaise longue, then made my way to the airport. Not long after, I found myself flying Holmes and Krüger to London in the monoplane of a friend of my uncle's pilot friend, le Comte de Saint-Exupéry. I didn't ask Holmes if he knew the count was part of the French Resistance.

The fuselage of the Fokker Tri-Motor was enclosed, but the fabric did little to reduce the atmospheric chill or dampen the propeller drone and engine gutturals. Still, Krüger slept through the flight, swathed in a duvet. For more than a decade, I'd craved his blood as a snowbird craves cocaine; but he was shrunken and pathetic where he huddled in a passenger seat. And he was defanged— the viper turned as powerless as a worm.

I supposed my uncle, who must be equally exhausted, would join the scientist in sleep. Then his fingertips brushed the sleeve of my leather pilot's jacket, recovered with other items from my covert Berlin bolt-hole.

I turned to the co-pilot's seat, and the intense regard of his storm-coloured eyes.

"You weren't surprised by Dr Krüger's presence aboard the *Victoria*. Clearly, Churchill wanted the enemy scientist brought back alive from the earth's core to serve Britain. It's ugly Realpolitik," he said. "But it's not a reason you'd betray England, Lucy."

I relived the moment again, as I knew not how many times I had before: An falling, the crack of the Webley revolver, M's bullet in the back of her head.

"My dear uncle," I answered, "I suggest you ask M how he feels about killing an innocent woman in cold blood."

Pallor spread over my uncle's face like a stain.

"Though neither English nor ally," I said, "the woman yet aided the British Empire. She was repaid with execution."

He made no reply, and I focused on flying, letting myself dissolve into the timeless immediacy of the air.

We were approaching the English Channel when he spoke again.

"Russia's royals would have fallen without British protection, I told myself. And why should England not seize control of Germany and Austria, when they invaded their neighbours and precipitated a worldwide war?"

For a moment, I was befuddled. Then I realised Holmes was reviving our conversation about the alien occupation of England.

"Then we invaded Belgium and France," he said, "and I began to ask myself." In the afternoon light, his expression grew sombre as dusk. "What right had we to conquer our own allies?"

I gave no answer.

I felt the aëroplane around us—the pressure of her rudder-bar against my soles, the flex of her muscles, the shiver of her skin, the vibration of her motors, the wind beneath her wings. Even had they not killed me a couple of times—even had I never set foot in one—it would be easy to understand how aëroplanes end so often in crashes, in flames, in fatalities. What faith a fragile mortal must have, to take to the sky in a frail wood and fabric shell, with a pilot he had so recently seemed eager to destroy.

"Now we plan the conquest of other worlds, and I can fool myself no longer," Holmes said, in the hoarse voice of a man who's just lost his best friend. "We're no better than the aliens who invaded England."

"Uncle—"

I fell silent as he turned to me, his expression suddenly as fierce as an eagle's.

"Lucy," he said, "the Americans must be warned of Britain's interplanetary ambitions—and the people of the moon, Venus, and Mars, as well."

My heart lifted like the aëroplane of my first solo flight as it rose to the dawn, but I said only, "Your thought is mine, uncle."

"We don't have access to one of the trans-aethereal Gridley wireless devices, do we."

It wasn't a question, but I answered. "The United States retains that secret."

"I don't know how we might warn the Selenites," Holmes said. "But I know some of Napier's friends from his rocket-car days in Berlin, and his friend in Los Angeles. They've been in covert communication with him on Venus all along. And his American friend can convey word of Britain's extraterrestrial ambitions to Carter and Paxton on Mars, as well."

He opened his coat and pulled out a thin sheaf of papers. The sheets were folded but I could see enough of the penmanship to recognise his hand. I read some of the lines.

I drew a breath. "The space programme information from my story."

"Decoded," he said. "I'll ensure it reaches the United States."

I tried to say, "Thank you," but couldn't make a sound.

"I think I should also inform—" his gaze became sharp as volcanic glass "—everyone else."

My pulse was speeding like a Model J Duesenberg. "Clarimal and I wanted no nation to have an advantage," I said. "But we couldn't risk contacting multiple nations."

"It would have ensured your quick discovery as double agents," Holmes said. "But everyone expects the world's first consulting detective to have worldwide contacts."

"Nothing would please Miss Stein or me better than for you to share the information with your friends."

I didn't add that we also had widespread contacts to whom we might give the information. I expected him to deduce this and say so. But his next words were a surprise.

"You and Miss Stein need to disappear."

"Everyone must believe us dead," I said, "save my mother."

My mother's voice recalls me to the present, where I've admitted myself to her town house in defiance of all etiquette.

"Lucy?"

My mother is concerned. Without knowing my assignment, she knows I shouldn't be in England now. Certainly, I shouldn't be visiting after midnight. But her manners are impeccable, as if I'm answering an invitation to tea.

"To what do I owe the pleasure of your company?"

I set my shoulders. "Mother, you once said I shouldn't apologise for telling you the truth."

"Why should I want you to lie to me?"

"You're about to find out."

Luana Island, Pellucidar

Under a swollen sun, my mate and I sit on the ledge of a sheer cliff, far above the sea. Bees and hummingbirds dart about us, visiting flowers which paint the air with a dizzying palette of scents, sweet as strawberries, spicy as cinnamon, sharp as wine. Some blooms are bigger than my head, and others are petite as a ladybird. Most are vibrant shades — red and yellow, orange and purple — but the small bloom I place in Clarimal's hair is white, shading inwardly to faint pink.

From the ledge, we can see a long way, but no horizon is visible. Instead, the seascape curves upwards, fading into the hazy blue atmosphere of Pellucidar, the primordial world on the inner surface of the Hollow Earth. We might be within a great bubble of water, with dinosaurs skimming or breaking the surface on every side. Given the abundance of carnivores, we keep our backs against the cliff.

Clarimal points with her stone-tipped spear. "There's a flock drawing near."

I raise my Bergmann machine rifle. "Haven't seen those cat-sized beasts before. They look part pterosaur and part auk."

"And part shark, to judge by their teeth."

They swoop away with feline grace, to our relief. Size is irrelevant to danger, and dangers are legion in Pellucidar. One does not voluntarily go anywhere here without abundant weaponry.

Clarimal and I came to the Hollow Earth with the American inventor Gridley's expedition, which flew from Germany in his experimental airship and utilised the northern polar entrance. When Clarimal and I left the expedition, we proceeded to An the Mezop's homeland. Her people had offered us a place in their community for bringing them news of her fate, though they know we're "blood spirits." We'll return eventually to the earth's surface, but for now Clarimal and I live on the cliff, away from the Mezops' village. Supernatural beings breed unease. Keeping mostly to ourselves is easier on everyone.

On the ledge between us, our battery-operated transaethereal Gridley radio murmurs. It's adapted to receive wireless broadcasts on the conventional frequencies. The BBC Empire Service is concluding its lead news story.

Clarimal says, "It sounds as if every nation on earth is building an atomic spaceship."

"Perhaps they are," I say. "We provided the details of Britain's space programme to newspapers around the world."

"And, perhaps, the nations use that information to pursue the dream of the atomic bomb," she says. "We must hope the nations come to stalemate, instead of mutual destruction."

The news continues, informing us that English writer Christopher Isherwood, an Austrian citizen named Clarimal Stein, and Lucy Harker, the daughter of Dracula's slayer, perished tragically in a single-vehicle accident in rural Prussia.

In an unrelated story, German science criminal Dr Krüger is on trial for war crimes, and Sherlock Holmes has testified.

The trial is a sensation. It has revealed Britain's secret use of German war scientists, along with Churchill's role in their recruitment, and his "black budget" for covert actions unknown even to Parliament, funded by secret gold from the earth's core. Churchill has resigned, and many are demanding he be put on trial. Many also call for England's most trusted man to be made prime minister, a notion which must fill Sherlock Holmes with horror.

Separately, the BBC has reported the sudden retirement of Mr Mycroft Holmes from government service and public life, citing his health and advanced years.

I had thought my mother would not leave M and would not speak to me again. My expectations were partially incorrect. She saw me again before my return to Germany and Clarimal.

She said, "Only my husband is to blame for his actions."

As we parted, perhaps never to see each other again, I offered my cheek for her kiss.

She astonished me with an embrace which threatened to snap ribs and shatter vertebrae.

"Be safe in Pellucidar," she said, "and happy with Miss Stein."

Clarimal's voice breaks gently into my thoughts.

"You're pensive, darling." She snaps off the BBC broadcast and rests her hand on mine. "We've left so many behind."

She doesn't mean only the friends and family, lovers and ex-lovers, who think us dead. She is thinking of her aging renfield, Frau Rudolph, who declined to accompany

Clarimal to this ageless world in favor of retirement to her homeland. Clarimal also remembers beloved mortals lost to age and death across the centuries, and the women she slew in the early, mad years of her vampirism.

"There are things," she murmurs, "that we may never know."

"I, too, hope the golden people never return to Earth."

My mate's eyes hold mine as her lips brush the back of my hand, light as the edge of a butterfly's wing. I draw her closer.

Waking, I realise that Clarimal and I drifted to sleep after our passion. I take up my machine rifle and look for dangers. They prove as bountiful as treasure in a pirate's dream, and as indifferent.

Clarimal sleeps among the flowers like a mortal, with relaxed face and regular breaths. We have her coffin, but she doesn't seem to need it here. There is no dawn or sunset at the earth's core; there is no night. Only eternal noon.

When she opens her eyes, I smile. "Nothing's chosen us for dinner at the moment."

I provide unneeded assistance as she sits up. A breeze stirs, rippling the fur of our discarded tunics and caressing our bare skin. Our loose hair unfurls like silk streamers. My hair looks odd. I draw a lock to its full length.

When we fell asleep, my hair reached no farther than the points of my shoulder-blades.

"I've slept only three times at the earth's core," I say with a laugh. "Yet my hair has grown to my hips, as if I were a shorn vampire with her tresses restored by a day in her coffin."

"Time plays strange tricks where the sun never moves." Clarimal tugs one of my locks gently. "I'll bob your hair."

"It's been long for much of my life," I say. "Why change on the brink of eternity?"

"Eternity?" My mate's expression turns grim. "You cannot have forgotten that the soulless end in ashes and dust."

I smile. "But not just yet."

Her expression grows more sombre, and I hear again her despairing cry in the shadow of obliteration. *Would that I'd destroyed your soul when I had the chance—*

Sobering, I take her hand. "There will be no better chance."

Clarimal studies my expression for what seems an eternity. I hear the vital spate of her blood quickening in its channels. Finally, she slips her arm around my shoulders and draws me closer. But the smile which touches her lips is melancholy.

"You don't know what you ask, Lucy Harker," she says quietly. "But it is your decision to make."

I lean closer, pressing the back of her hand to my breast. "One final consideration, Clarimal."

Her soft tone is intimate as a kiss. "What is it, darling?"

I smile. "I've yearned for decades to learn if the rumours about the unparalleled pleasure of Carmilla's bite are true."

Gently, Clarimal brushes my lips with hers.

When she draws back, there is only warmth in her smile. "I cannot say," she answers. "You'll need to tell me, darling."

Then she bends to my neck.

About the Author

Cynthia Ward has published stories in *Analog*, *Asimov's*, *Black Cat Mystery*, *Nightmare*, *Weird Tales*, and other magazines and anthologies. She edited *Lost Trails: Forgotten Tales of the Weird West* Volumes 1-2 (WolfSinger Publications). With Charles G. Waugh and Jeffrey Linscott, she coedited *Weird Trails* (Sam Teddy Publishing). With Nisi Shawl, Cynthia cocreated the Writing the Other fiction workshop and coauthored *Writing the Other: A Practical Approach* (Aqueduct Press), which were honored with a Locus Award. The first book of her Blood-Thirsty Agent series, *The Adventure of the Incognita Countess* (Aqueduct), was a finalist for the Gaylactic Spectrum Award for Best Novel.